S0-AFN-079

Misconception

Also by Ryan Boudinot

The Littlest Hitler

Misconception

A ~~Memoir~~ Novel

Ryan Boudinot

Black Cat
New York
a paperback original imprint of Grove Atlantic, Inc.

Published simultaneously in Canada
Printed in the United States of America

FIRST EDITION

ISBN: 978-0-8021-7065-1

Black Cat
a paperback original imprint of Grove/Atlantic, Inc.
841 Broadway
New York, NY 10003

Distributed by Publishers Group West

www.groveatlantic.com

09 10 11 12 13   10 9 8 7 6 5 4 3 2 1

To my mother and father.

The Pacific Northwest.

I was suspended in eighth grade for bringing my semen to science class. We were supposed to inspect living things under the microscope. Mrs. Wheeler had used the example of pond water. My friend Paul Dills's sample was a minnow that had eaten itself to death. Other kids brought leaves, feathers, dirt, hair. The morning of the assignment I whacked off into a Tupperware Popsicle mold. On the way to school, I revealed the contents of my plain brown paper sack to Paul as we hacked on his aunt's menthol cigarettes under the bridge. First, Paul expressed amazement that I had experienced an orgasm. Second, that I'd thought to bring attention to this fact in science class. Third, that I expected to ace the assignment with it.

There were three students at each work station. My partners were Paul and Rachel Hilden, one of the kids who'd brought a jar of murky pond water. Rachel had accumulated a tragic assortment of nicknames, among the most recent, Toilet Paper Stuck to Shoe Bitch. Her mouth, reengineered with scaffolding and rubber bands, had allegedly been the subject of a research paper in an orthodontia journal. Though she would grow up to become vengefully gorgeous and anchor an Idaho news show, in eighth grade she was prone to postlunch fishing trips in the Dumpsters to recover missing retainers. I doubted Rachel knew that semen existed.

We inspected Rachel's pond water first, taking turns peering at the boring blobs. Then we looked at Paul's minnow bacteria and saw a few crawly things. I used a Q-tip to dab a slide with my substance.

"What did you bring, Cedar?" Rachel said.

By the way, I was named after a tree.

"I brought baby tadpoles," I said.

"That's not tadpoles. That's spit."

I loaded the slide and turned the dial to 200x magnification. I'd often examined the photos of sperm cells in my dog-eared masturbation material, *Our Bodies, Ourselves,* and watched footage of wriggling sperm on PBS, but these sperm were special: they had originated in my testes, each one trafficking my genetic material in its top-heavy little head. They had been designed to withstand the arduous trip into a uterus, but few had survived my two-mile bike ride to school. Even dead they were fascinating to look at, each a tiny exclamation point carrying my half of what could have been a human being.

"Let me see!" Paul said. When I moved away he squinted into the instrument and his jaw slowly sagged. "They have tails and everything! Holy crap!"

Paul's excitement quickly attracted the attention of nearby work stations. He was bad at keeping secrets, and was probably the last guy in class I should have told about my semen sample. Everyone wanted to take a look. Kat Daniels stepped up and brushed a few strands of hair from her face as she bent to peer into the battered middle school microscope. By our rudimentary, junior high standards, Kat wasn't counted among the prettiest girls at our school. She had a slightly upturned nose that would have looked awkward if it weren't for the sleepy eyes hanging over it. She wore chipped, sparkly fingernail polish. Her beauty was slowly unfolding, refracted through my growing capability to notice her. As she squinted into the microscope, there passed an interminably nervous moment occupied by her, me, and millions of reproductive cells. She was quiet a moment. I watched her understand. Then she looked up and said, "Cool."

After that I didn't care how grody I was in the eyes of my classmates. Kat slithered back to her station to study a daisy. In an instant, everyone was crouching over my sample, the guys exclaiming and the girls making retching noises. Mrs. Wheeler peeled her face from an Agatha Christie novel and slammed down her coffee cup. Everyone scattered. Our teacher peered into the microscope long enough to determine the nature of my sample, then pointed in the direction of the door. "Mr. Warner's office. Now."

As I walked stiffly from the room, Rachel Hilden pressed her eye against the microscope. "Whoa," she said. "These tadpoles really *are* miniature."

Mr. Warner, tapping a ruler against his knee, sat on the corner of his wood-grain, Formica-topped desk in a way that must have stimulated his anus. Individual fibers of polyester in his tan Sansabelt pants audibly creaked when he shifted from one buttock to the other.

"Human sexuality is what we're talking about here," he said. "Poets? Yeah sure they wrote about it, scientists have performed serious research into it, heck, some of the world's greatest paintings depict figures of the nudes and what have you." He leaned closer and leveled his ruler at me. "But based on the undistinguished year you've had at this institution of learning I can only conclude that these kinds of fancy thoughts were not what you had in mind when you pulled your grotesque little stunt."

Mrs. Wheeler sat in the other visitor's chair, the paper bag with the offending specimen on the desk before her. A dark brown patch grew larger as my semen leaked through a corner of the bag.

I hoped Mr. Warner wouldn't make me call my mom. He leaned closer. "Everyone's sexual maturity has to start somewhere, Cedar. Do you really want yours to start like this? The mistakes you make now, when it comes to sex, will shape the rest of your experiences. Do you want to become a pervert? A homosexual? Cedar, are your parents exposing you to pornography?" he said quietly.

"Right," I said. "I *wish*."

The principal sighed, displaying a theatrical sort of disappointment. "It looks like in light of some of your recent unexcused absences, your role as ring leader in February's biscuits-and-gravy lunch-room walkout, and this *sperm* business, you've left me no other choice but to issue a week's suspension." As if to add a little ceremony to his decision, Mr. Warner picked up the bag and dropped it into his waste can. A string of semen dangling from the bag fell across his left knee.

My father was Wade Rivers, a name as dumb as mine. That afternoon he arrived home early, took two steps into the kitchen, and threw his briefcase against the refrigerator. The magnetic letters spelling profanities limited by five lousy vowels skittered to the floor in clumps. A picture of me taken with my mom's fish-eye lens floated to the linoleum as the freezer door swung open, releasing a carton of Neapolitan, a tray of ice cubes, and an inadequately-sealed bag of frozen peas. My dad's briefcase popped open and scattered his hectic legal scribblings. He swore. He kicked cabinetry. Apparently he'd lost another case. Helping him pick up the mess seemed the most sensible course of action. I had seen my father this angry before, many times, and knew that the best thing to do was to eradicate the stunned silence by being productive. I began gathering his papers and re-adhering magnets to the fridge. My dad sighed, bent down, said, "Shit, no, no, I'll get that," then saw that the cardboard flap of the ice-cream carton had been left open.

"Have I or have I not explained the concept of freezer burn to you?" my dad said.

"I'll eat it."

"Not helpful, Cedar. Now nobody else can enjoy it, and you'll only eat it to make a point."

"I'm sorry you lost your case." This is what I thought I was supposed to say, so I said it. My dad shrugged. "Also, I got suspended."

"What for?"

"We had an experiment where we had to bring something from nature to look at under a microscope."

"And you brought—"

"Sperm?"

My father sat down at the kitchen table and considered the pig-shaped salt and pepper shakers. Finally he said, "Please at least tell me it was your own sperm."

"It was," I said. Then my mom came home.

My mother, her name was Janet, was a medical photographer who documented abrasions, growths, and autopsy oddities for the university hospital. In my house, Frank Netter's classic text *Atlas of Human Anatomy* was coffee-table material. We had a model skull named Barbara on our mantle. My mother and I had a standing arrangement that whenever I had an abrasion or ingrown toenail I'd be sure to show her. Most families kept photo albums of birthday snapshots. Ours contained a few vacation shots and photographic proof of bicycle accidents, blisters, pustulant sties.

My parents met when my dad was starting out as a public defender and my mom worked for the county coroner. Their courtship revolved around a spectacular triple homicide that rocked our county in the early seventies. My mom recorded the crime scene and subsequent autopsies. My dad admitted years later that her grisly pictures were what had swayed the jury. She often told me that if the murderer had gotten off, she would have never forgiven my father. I was lucky: the guy was sentenced to death; I was conceived.

My mother, striding through the front door with her swaying camera bag, praising a particularly photogenic teratoma: "From the outside it looked like any other tumor, but in dissection we found *hair* and *teeth* and I think even a fingernail or two."

"Go ahead, tell her," my dad said, confronting the refrigerator for a beer.

"I got suspended for looking at sperm under a microscope."

"Clarification. His *own* sperm."

"*Cedar*," my mom said, then turned to my dad, "Did you remember to make ice cubes?"

"Yeah, you want an iced tea?"

"I'll make it," my mom said. "I mean really, Cedar. Sperm?"

"I wanted to know what they looked like."

My mother opened the freezer and twisted the ice cube tray until it yielded its cubes. "Who left the ice cream open?"

"You were expressing curiosity in human physiology," my dad said, leading the witness.

"Human physiology, huh?" my mom said. "If that was the case, why didn't you just use the microscope we bought you last Christmas?"

"It was me who left the ice cream open," I said.

"Don't try to change the subject," my mom said. "We're talking about sperm, not ice cream. Jesus, did we miss the deadline for the masturbation conversation, is that what this is about?"

"I've told him a hundred times about freezer burn!" my dad shouted.

"My microscope doesn't have good enough magnification," I said.

My mom said, "Cedar, we're not mad at you for wanting to understand the workings of your own body. But what were you thinking? It was Mrs. Wheeler's class, right? Christ, she drives a VW Rabbit with a Mamas and the Papas bumper sticker. She teaches a bread-making class at the community college! How did you expect her to react? My point is that if you want to look at your own sperm under a microscope, I can introduce you to some lab techs at the fertility clinic who'll leave you alone in a closet with a *Juggs* magazine and water-based lubricant and you can look at your own sperm under a microscope until the cows come home."

"Really?" my dad said, "They only had *Playboy* when I was there."

In truth, I had observed my sperm under my own microscope many times. I had witnessed their mass extinction suspended above the heat of the bulb, hunted for the oddball spermatozoa with two heads or tails, gazed myopically into the mystery of my chromosomal output. The secret reason for my act of scientific inquiry unraveled before me like the paper vortex of a Chinese yo-yo. I had taken the sperm to class to perform an experiment, certainly, but not the one that had been assigned. My experiment had proceeded from the hypothesis that if I were bold enough to offer forth my sperm as proof of my virility, I would win Kat's heart. After all, she was the girl who had approached me at my locker after my oral report on the state of Rhode Island and breathed two fantastic, incandescent words into my ear, "*I'm ovulating.*"

My parents drafted a list of chores for me to complete during my one-week suspension, but I still had time to read, shoot hoops, and masturbate in every room of the house while they were at work. Every day around three o'clock Paul would stop by on his way home and brief me on the shifting alliances and petty grudges of our class-mates while we shared his cigarettes behind the garage. On the last day of my suspension Paul crashed his bike into our hedge and declared, "Kat *has the slide.* She took it from the science lab and keeps it in her jewelry box!"

I demanded that he reveal his sources. Kat's friend Margot had told him, making him promise not to tell me, knowing that he would.

I said, "I'm going to need one of your cigarettes."

"You're in luck. I've got menthols."

We went around back behind the garage and conducted our adolescent tobacco ceremony.

"You think this means she wants me to call her?" I wondered.

"Call her? Cedar! Come to your senses. She wants you to bang her!"

That night I tried willing my mind into clairvoyance, desperate to know what Kat was doing that very moment, twenty blocks away. She was tucking my sperm into a little velvet-lined jewelry box among her rings and friendship pins. She was sneaking peeks at the slide as she did her homework, holding it up to the light of her bedside lamp. I conducted conversations with her in my head while I scraped moss off the deck, alphabetized the LPs, pulled rocks and weeds from the garden. I created a twenty-item list of conversation starters in case she called, but she remained as silent as me.

After a long and boring weekend I returned to school. Before I made it to my locker I learned that I'd been tagged with a number of nicknames that Paul hadn't had the heart to reveal. Post-it notes had been inserted into my locker through those slots the manufacturer must have included to avoid the liabilities of suffocated nerds. Wanker, Jizzmaster, Spermy. I wadded the notes into a ball and stuffed it deep behind a month-old lunch bag.

The final week of junior high school washes the blood from the most culpable of children's hands. My science class transgression was relegated to lore by other scandals —the Kevin Johnson pot bust, a girls' locker room raid, petty theft from Mrs. Wheeler's purse. Just over the hump of the academic calendar were neighborhood lawns to mow, each a counter-clockwise mandala generating the most beautiful aroma of summer. Emboldened by the freedom of the year's end, I called Kat the night after the last day of school, prepared with my list of topics and subtopics should our dialogue come to any awkward pauses. I didn't refer to the list once. We were like this diagram of bacteria entering a nostril I'd seen in one of my mom's medical books, nodes glomming onto receptors, spreading something virulent. I plundered Kat's opinions about our classmates, our teachers, the media products that had located us through TV, radio, and the multiplex. But I hesitated broaching the subject of the sperm that had brought us together. Now that we had entered the codified process of courtship—fake insults, overwrought pronouncements, long stretches of breathy silence between phone receivers deep into the night—now that we were falling for each other, it felt like a transgression to mention testosterone, ovulation, or spermatozoa sandwiched between layers of glass.

I slowly shoved breakfast at my face as my parents orbited the kitchen table, inserting themselves into my periphery with gentle threats of punishment for undone tasks and admonitions about how I chose to spend my lawn-mowing money. How pathetic their domestic regulations, how trivial were their to-do lists, when one could sup from the pond of the infinite in the sound of a sigh transmitted over a phone line. My dad apparently won an important case and I observed myself talking to him about it, prompting the man with questions at periodic silences. My mother showed me some photos she had taken of a diseased pancreas and I reacted as I suspected she wanted me to, with feigned sick fascination.

I mowed Mr. Dickman's yard, chopping up bits of cedar shingles ripped from his roof during a remodel, splattering piles of Saint Bernard shit. Mr. Dickman, shirtless, drinking a wine cooler, watched me from the window of his living room, which he had converted into his bedroom, as was the prerogative of a bachelor. I think he was some kind of public accountant but I'd never thought to ask. He occasionally entertained his busty Italian girlfriend, nuzzling her on the weather-beaten lawn furniture of his patio, slurping cocktails inappropriate to consume when enjoying a view consisting of the back of a bowling alley. When my lawn-care duties brought me in contact with the couple, they were usually feeding on Ritz crackers turded yellow with EZ Cheez and planting hickeys on each other's leathery necks. I went out of my way to chop up a lot of slugs with the weed whacker, spraying their guts on Mr. Dickman's deteriorating siding. When Mr. Dickman wasn't distracting me by using his rowing machine in the driveway, the drone of the mower lulled me into a meditative state in which I enumerated the obstacles between my and Kat's naked bodies.

When Kat and I finally managed to see each other at the mall a week after school got out, we held hands and walked a sober lap past the food court and jewelry stores like players in an ultraserious form of Japanese theater. Later, we made out in the back row during a matinee, after which our parents picked us up in their respective vehicles. We both had strict curfews and expectations about our physical locations, both answering to the strategies of animals regulating the fertility of their young.

Kat's parents were divorced. Her mother worked for a company that made yarn for craft stores, and her father repaired septic systems on the other side of the state. Kat also complained about her mother's boyfriend of two or three years, an older man who sounded like he had a lot of money.

Kat's mother forbade her from meeting me in any place that was not public. One night I arranged to stay at Paul's while she arranged to stay a block away at Margot's house. Paul had a detached garage with an upstairs where his pack-rat family stored beaten-up furniture they meant to eventually reupholster and resell, including a couch large enough for two people to stretch out on if one was on top of the other.

At one o'clock in the morning Kat emerged from a rhodedendron hedge, and in the bluish indirect light of a street lamp I helped pick sticky flower petals from her hair. I didn't know if I was supposed to kiss her at this point, so I offered her a piece of Big Red.

"Not that I think your breath is gross or anything," I said.

Paul motioned for us to be quiet, then showed us up the exterior steps of the garage to the loft, the kind of place we envisioned Fonzie living in. He left us alone.

I remember Kat putting me in her mouth. I couldn't figure out what I was supposed to be feeling. There were a lot of teeth involved and then nothing happened. I didn't want to hurt her feelings so I made some pleasure-related noises. And then in the half-dark she let me look upon the origin of the universe between her legs. Years later I would occasionally think of this moment when fucking my girlfriends.

Kat had preserved my sperm in a secret compartment beneath her bracelets and necklaces, but it wasn't released that night, or any of the subsequent moments we managed to steal from our unsuspecting parents. Maybe my body didn't yet understand what an orgasm with another person was supposed to mean. For whatever reason, I couldn't come. On the couch that night we were just tongues, patches of warmed denim, a cold nipple pressed into the intersection of the life line and love line of a boy's hand. We arrived at a pause. My balls ached.

"Is it okay I didn't, you know, come?" I said.

"I think so."

"Did you come?"

"It started feeling lots better but then, I don't know."

I pulled my sweatshirt down over her shoulders. She seemed disappointed.

"I can try again." I said.

"It's not that. It's not you. I just can't stop thinking about my mom and George. They want me to go with them on this idiotic boat trip to Alaska."

"How long will you be gone?"

"The whole month of July."

"Oh."

"I don't think I'll make it," she said. "Just think of me in that stupid boat with George the perv and me puking over the side. Maybe I can get a doctor's note that I'll get too seasick. Maybe I can stay at Margot's and be with you every night."

"I want to sleep next to you," I said. "I want to wake up with you."

"Promise me," she said.

In the weeks before the trip, Kat used some babysitting money to buy a microscope of her own. While other couples our age traded notes and broken-heart lockets, we furtively exchanged slides, my sperm for her vaginal mucosa. In the parking lot behind theater nine two weeks before she set sail, she presented me with a little box wrapped in an exchange student's origami paper.

"Swear you won't open it until you get home," Kat said. A stream of blinking people exited a matinee. "That's my mom's car. I gotta go."

I waited until she was out of sight before I peeled open the package. In the box I found a slide imprinted with a single droplet of blood. It burned a dark mystery in my pocket as I hurried home. That night, in my room, I peered into my microscope, hoping to discover the one thing on the mind of every one of my sperm: Kat's egg.

One night after playing Nintendo at Paul's I came home to find my parents sitting quietly at the kitchen table. Before I could make it to the fridge, my mom said, "I was looking for my scissors in your room and found these instead."

My dad pulled from his pocket a half-consumed pack of Camel Lights and set them on the table.

"Are you smoking?" my mother said.

"They're Paul's. He told me to hang on to them for him."

"So what did I smell in your room the other night?"

"I already told you. I lit a stick of deodorant on fire."

"Fair enough," my father said. "Let's see what burning deodorant smells like." He reached into his coat pocket and pulled out my stick of Brut. "Was this the kind of deodorant you did your experiment on?"

"Yeah."

My dad unscrewed the deodorant cap then struck a kitchen match and held it to the green dome in which a single armpit hair was embedded. The surface ignited easily, sending up a blue flame. The hair flared and turned to soot. My dad sniffed the air and turned to my mom. "Is this what you smelled the other night in Cedar's room?"

"No."

"According to Cedar, your sense of smell must have deceived you. Is that what you're telling us, Cedar?"

"I dunno," I said, picking at the rubber sole of one of my Chuck Taylor's with a ballpoint.

"On to exhibit B." From the laundry room my father fetched one of my sweatshirts, which he held to my mother's nose. "What does this smell like to you?"

"Cigarette smoke," my mom said flatly.

"Jesus! Paul and I went to Denny's and sat in the smoking section. Big deal."

"Cedar. Quit bullshitting us," my mom said. "We know you started smoking. And it's going to stop tonight. Do you understand?"

"*Yes.*"

"You *know* what smoking does to your body. But in case you forgot, let me show you."

My mother emptied a manila folder, spreading pictures of blackened lungs across the table. "These are real people's

20

bodies, Cedar. This is what the inside of a smoker's body looks like. This is supposed to be *pink*."

As they delivered their lecture, I focused my attention on the glossies. I wasn't going to give them the satisfaction of thinking I'd been swayed. I'd heard this kind of patronizing shit before, at a school assembly, delivered by hospital volunteers who dressed as lungs and sang a song about emphysema. My parents didn't need to show me pictures to convince me that the inside of a human body was a sacred, incredible place. I had seen blood cells, I had watched sperm die. I had touched the mollusk protuberance of a cervix.

Then I saw the picture of a girl, her body cavity opened from neck to navel, her organs scooped out, an empty canyon between her young breasts. Her slack-jawed head lolled to one side.

"She was your age," my mom said. The floor underneath me appeared to tilt a little. I held onto the table and for a moment lost my sense of vision. A little vomit climbed up my throat then burned its way back down. When I opened my eyes again my mom was dabbing my forehead with a cold dish cloth. "I forget how upsetting those sorts of pictures can be," she said.

"Let me see it again," I said. She showed me. Looking at it made me wonder the same sorts of things I wondered when viewing pornography, like where did this person live, what were they doing hours before this revealing photo-graph was taken, what did their house look like, did their families know. I filled my lungs with air and let it out slowly. "What happened to her?"

"She killed herself drinking industrial solvent."

"Fuck," I said. "Why do you show me these things?"

"So you won't forget you're mortal."

In Kat's neighborhood the elms had lived long enough to entwine their branches above the street like praying hands. I parked my bike against a tree and considered not ringing the doorbell of their split-level. I could still blow off their invitation to dinner. Kat answered the door, quickly kissed me, and led me by the hand up the stairs into the kitchen where her mother was preparing the meal. Veronica looked older than my mom, which startled me. She wore lots of beads, a head wrap, a loose yellow sweater that hung from her body in a manner that suggested she advocated women's lib.

"Welcome to our madness," Veronica said, stirring pasta in a metal bowl, then laughed when I didn't respond. "Oh, grab a soda. There's Sprite and Tab. I hope you like pasta 'cause that's what we're having. I grew the tomatoes for the sauce myself."

"Her sauce is awesome," Kat said.

"You have a nice house," I said.

"This dump? Please. We've got dry rot, wet rot, the pipes freeze every winter and this summer it looks like we have ourselves a ladybug infestation."

Kat exhaled and slumped against the refrigerator. "Gol, Mom, he's only trying to give you a compliment."

"Come to think of it, it is kind of a dump," I said.

We laughed. Veronica's boyfriend George clomped stiffly up the stairs. He was an angular format of a human being with tiny eyes in the kind of bald head that seems to automatically come with a mustache. He wore a necktie tucked under a cardigan sweater vest. I couldn't tell whether this was his standard at-home attire or if he had just returned from somewhere more formal. Kat had told me George worked with computers at a bank. He shook my hand and some featureless words got lost between us among clanging dishes. Veronica set the table with the pasta, bread, salad, and a bowl of steamed broccoli and we took our seats under a dimmed fixture.

"Let us say grace," George said, grasping my hand, squeezing my fingers against a gigantic class ring. He bowed his head, closed his eyes, then arched his eyebrows upward. "Oh Heavenly Father we ask that you bless this food with the blood of thy son Christ Jesus. We offer our everlasting praise as you nourish and nurture us in body, mind, and soul. And Heavenly Father we welcome our guest with the fruit of thy bounty the Lord our Savior. May you guide these young people in their budding relationship and bar them from temptation. For as their lust is strong so shall you give them the strength to not go past first base. Ah-men."

"*Amen.*"

"So," Veronica said, passing the broccoli to me, "I understand you're the reason Kat has become so interested in science."

I said my own little silent prayer that they hadn't seen my slides in her jewelry box. "It's my best subject," I explained. "I like thinking about how living things work."

"Like biology?" George said.

"Sure. I'm most interested in what happens at the cellular level."

"So you believe in evolution," George said.

I looked at Kat to see how I should respond. She speared her broccoli.

"Sure."

"Hmm. Well I do, too, to an extent. But how come the seas don't have more salt if they're so old? No one's been able to answer that one."

"So I guess you're going on a big trip," I said.

"That's correct," said George, "Can't wait to get out on the water with the orcas and the sunshine and the foam splashing across the bowsprit. I guess you could say I've always been a seaman at heart."

"A what at heart?" Kat said.

Veronica interrupted, "Cedar, do you like music by the band Black Sabbath?"

George wiped his face and leaned back in his chair. "Oh, honey, you're not going to pollute this young man's mind with that trash."

"It's not trash, it's part of my life. Maybe I've grown up and moved on to Ashford and Simpson and Peter Cetera but at one time I was what they called a go-go dancer and dang proud of it."

"You danced for Black Sabbath?" I said.

"Ozzy Osbourne autographed her butt," Kat said.

"That's enough," George said.

"What music did you listen to when you were . . ." I asked George.

"When I was what, young? You calling me a dinosaur? Hey, I personally own *Sports* by Huey Lewis and the News. And you might be surprised to know that on weekends I wear Jordache jeans. But since you asked, there were a whole slew of groups I enjoyed back when I was a greaser. The Platters, Four Tops, Paul Revere and the Raiders, you name it. I grooved down to it all."

"'Ozzy' on one cheek, 'Osbourne' on the other," Kat whispered.

Veronica frowned. "What does your family usually talk about at the dinner table, Cedar?"

"Homicides."

"Cedar's parents—" Kat started.

"I know what Cedar's parents do," George said. "I understand your old man is a public defender. Must be difficult. How come he didn't go into prosecution? All those sleazeballs he has to represent."

"He wanted to make sure everyone got fair representation in our system. Not just people who can afford it. And he wanted to defend the innocent."

"Can someone please pass the margarine?" Kat said.

"What about the ones he *knows* aren't innocent? What do you do when you've got a guy you know *deserves* to get locked up but you help put him back out on the street? Maybe it's just me, but I don't see how a guy could live with himself defending some of those creeps."

Veronica leveled a knife at her boyfriend. "If you have any other questions about Cedar's father, you might consider asking him instead."

George shrugged. "It's a philosophical question."

"So what route are you taking on your trip?" I said.

"We'll be going up around Vancouver Island, to Ketchikan, Skagway, a bunch of other Indian names I can't remember. We'll make a stop in Port Hardy, which, I just found this out today, was founded by a survivor of the Titanic."

"You think it's a good idea to talk about the Titanic before you go on a boat trip?" Kat said.

I twirled linguine around my fork and kept misjudging how much I could eat in one bite. The whorl of pasta kept growing larger than bite-size, and I kept having to unroll it and start over again.

"What subjects are you taking in school next year, Cedar?" Veronica asked me.

"I think the basics. Geometry. State history," I said.

"Going out for any sports?" George said.

"Maybe golf or tennis."

"Of course. Doctor and lawyer sports. So you can play with your father."

"My dad doesn't play either. He swims."

"What about your mother? What does she do?" George said.

"She jogs."

"I mean for a *job*."

"She's a medical photographer."

"Now that's something I just couldn't do," Veronica said. "I can't even stand it when I see a run-over cat in the street."

"She says the trick is to not think of them as people anymore. They're just bodies. They're just systems and organs," I said.

Kat scrunched up her face.

"Yes, but what of the soul?" George said.

"I don't believe in a soul."

"And God? You don't believe in Him, either?"

"I guess, no, not really."

George shrugged. "That's odd, I could have sworn I heard you say *amen* a short bit ago."

Veronica pointed her knife again. "George, I'm serious. Stop with the inquisition. You're making our guest uncomfortable."

"Inquisition?" George said. "Cedar, am I making you uncomfortable?"

"No," I said.

"See?"

"What else is he going to say? God!" Kat said.

"I don't believe in God at all," I said.

George said, "And yet you believe in justice."

Veronica tried to interrupt, asking, "Who wants more bread?"

George continued, "Let's get down to brass tacks. You come over to dinner, pray with us without believing a word of it, then claim to believe in giving everyone a fair shake, yet have nothing to base it on, no eternal consequences for our earthly deeds. No God, no reason for being, just people trying to be *just* in a godless void. Not the kind of world I want to live in."

"What's wrong with being just?" I said.

"Nothing at all, friend," George said, "but justice without the power and grace of God backing it up is arbitrary. Makes no difference if you're *just* or not if you don't have

28

to answer to your deeds in the next life, if you believe in a next life at all. I feel sorry for you if that's the kind of world you think you live in."

"Who's up for watching my videotape?" Veronica said.

Kat stared at her food. A sharp glance passed from Veronica to George. I tried to fill the silence by digging the hole deeper. "I believe in things that can be proved. Or tested, like with the scientific method."

George laughed a loud "Ha!" and dabbed his chin with a napkin. "You have much to learn, son."

"I'd like it if you didn't call me son."

"Say again?"

"Don't insult my father, then call me *son*."

George slowly set down his knife and said, "I don't appreciate you coming to my house expecting to date my— Veronica's—daughter and telling me what I can or can't say, *son*."

Kat slapped her palm on the table. "Shut up, George. This is so not your house and you have no place making my boyfriend uncomfortable."

George threw his hands up and laughed. "What is this? Can't a guy have a conversation? Maybe at the Rivers household they talk about open-heart surgery and how to spring dope dealers out of jail, but here I'll talk about whatever I damn well please."

"George, you're being an asshole," Veronica said. After that the man did some grumbling and we consumed the rest of the meal amid the excruciating noises of silverware striking porcelain. When George left to work on his boat Veronica put her hand on my shoulder and said, "Cedar, I am so sorry. I don't know what his problem was tonight, he's usually not like this. Will you stick around for pie?"

We went into the living room with our apple pie à la mode. Veronica inserted a Betamax tape into the player.

"Kat thinks it's *soooo* embarrassing when I show this but I bet you'll get a kick out of it. This was when I lived in California."

What appeared on the TV was an early Black Sabbath music video, with lots of zooming camera action and swirly psychedelic colors. Over Ozzy Osbourne's right shoulder stood a platform on which a younger version of Veronica danced in a mini skirt and white go-go boots. As we watched the grainy tape, Kat occasionally buried her face in a throw pillow in mortification. During the slow-tempo bridge, the camera zoomed in on Veronica's young face. Years later, in a suburban living room, as Ozzy sang of children of the grave. She shook her head in wonderment.

Twenty years and
six months later;
Albany, New York.

Here's upstate New York, brutalized by a sadistic winter storm. Across the slippery parking lot of the Extended Stay hotel was a bar. From outside I recognized the muffled, pubic grunt of seventies rock. Inside, a gin and tonic was placed in front of me, capturing smeared bits of ESPN in the ice cubes. I waited for Kat. She had found me on the Internet and we'd arranged to meet in Albany. In her email she'd said she was writing a book in which I played a significant role and she needed me to read it and sign some legal documents giving her permission to publish it.

Earlier that day I had enjoyed a mimosa in a geothermal hot tub in Reykjavik. The storm made me nervous about getting stuck here too long. I was happiest en route, with my laptop and a coffee in a sleeved paper cup, arranging ground transportation, stepping from gate to plane to gate. Inhaling jet fumes in the optimism of rental-car parking lots. Now I was paused in a city bled by politics and punished with ice.

Kat and I noticed each other almost simultaneously, recognized one another a moment later. She existed. Her dyed hair concealed secret ex-hairstyles. Her eyes looked punched-in with eyeliner. She locked on my gaze hard, then looked away. Our personalities were no longer circumscribed by text, they were here in the physical world amid smoke and misshapen humans. We closed the space between us, meeting at a table with a guttering candle.

"You came," she said.

"Hi, Kat."

"And to the east coast, too."

"Yeah, weird. Meeting old, you know, people," I said.

"You're finally a real person again." She seemed to be making herself smile. "Once I got past the listings for retirement communities in Idaho, I was able to track down the real Cedar Rivers. But I never asked you where you were living."

"Silicon Valley. That sounds pretentious. Palo Alto or thereabouts. I work for this medical tech company. You already know that. From my email. You got it off the site. What about you? You moved, right? I got that postcard you sent from New Mexico years ago."

"Arizona. Yeah, after the southwest I got into school back east here. So I've moved around."

"Your mom?"

"Still in Arizona. She married a guy. Her third marriage."

"And George?"

"He died about eight, nine years ago. One of those random highway snipers. He wasn't the guy who was hit, though. He was driving *behind* the guy who was hit. So he hit the guy who was hit. It was in the news for a day. There's no pleasant way to spin it."

"Wow. I'm sorry to hear that. You never think of that kind of thing happening to an actual person," I said.

"You have no wedding ring. I thought you'd be married."

"Engaged."

"Congratulations."

"Thanks. Why are you in Albany I meant to ask. You traveling for business?" I said.

"Sort of. I was up here at an artist colony."

"Really. I don't know what that is."

"It's a place where artists go to get work done."

Kat traced fake wood grains on the Formica with an index finger. I was pleased to see she still wore black fingernail polish.

"You had a book of short stories published," I said.

"You've never heard of it. It came and went. Got a couple reviews."

"You're famous now, though, right?"

Kat laughed. "Name one other person who had a debut collection of short stories come out last year."

"I'd like to read it."

"You can get it online. Don't pay attention to the one-star reviews. Fuck, Cedar. I must be on drugs is what it feels like here. So, your job. I read a little about your company. Medical technology? I didn't really understand most of it."

I cleared my throat. "We develop web-based medical-imaging technology. You've seen the ads probably. Like when you see an actor playing a surgeon looking at a monitor, performing surgery on a patient thousands of miles away. That's a crude way of showing what we do. So far it's mostly sci-fi. I visit hospitals, give presentations. My title is chief medical officer, if you can believe it. I was just in Iceland. They're interested in hosting telemedicine sessions with clients from Europe and the States. Like I said in my email, boring. Or maybe it's exciting, I don't know. The company is taking a beating on the Street, looking for another round of financing. I travel a lot. But enough of that. A book! The one you're writing. I always assumed you'd be a painter."

"I started writing fiction as an undergrad, wrote a novel that's absolute shit. Went to grad school out here, got my MFA."

"That's Masters in . . ."

"Fucking and Alcoholism. Fine arts. It's where unpublished writers study under published writers, hoping to figure out how to get published. If they're really lucky they get jobs teaching other unpublished writers."

"Oh yeah? Who'd you study with."

"Some great people. Rick Moody."

"Never heard of him."

"Ever see *The Ice Storm*?"

"Vaguely rings a bell."

"That Frodo guy was in it."

"I guess I missed it."

"Sigourney Weaver?"

"I don't know. Jesus, now I have to read your stuff. This new book of yours."

"I came out here to write about what happened that summer."

"That's a vague way to put it."

"I'm not nearly as vague in the book."

"I guess that would make for a good story. I need another drink. I'm speaking for myself here. How're you doing, drinkwise?"

"This is just one in a series of cocktails."

I went to the bar and ordered another round. There was the exit, beckoning. Just walk toward the men's john and keep going out the back door. Thumb a cab to the airport. Sleep on a bench with airport CNN blaring overhead. I observed myself ordering another drink against my better judgment. Apparently, instead of catching the next flight to the Bay Area I was going to keep talking to this woman who possessed my most painful memories. When I returned to the table, I set my drink down, already half-finished.

Kat said, "So, your wife."

"My *fiancée*."

"That's what I meant."

"Her name is L. She has a website written from the point of view of our cat."

"You own a cat together?"

"I meant her cat."

Kat changed the subject again. "So, I asked you to come here because my editor says I need you to sign some legal bullshit promising you won't sue me when the memoir comes out."

"You're afraid there's material in your book that's slanderous."

"It's more complicated than that," Kat said. "Parts of it I wrote from your point of view."

In Kat's hotel room, I stepped over a case of wine and cleared a half-finished Sunday *Times* crossword from a chair. She offered an insincere apology for the mess. On the desk were the contents of a sack lunch: a cellophane-wrapped sandwich, an apple, carrot sticks. Some books—

In Cold Blood, something by Philip Roth. Her clothes all over the place. On the table sat a PowerBook. Toiletries and coffee supplies, a printer, a sleeping bag, CDs in sleeves, masking tape. Loose change. A lone tampon clawing its way out of its applicator. A pack of spearmint gum.

"I have to set up the printer," she said, digging through her laptop bag for a USB. "You want some vino? I don't think they're going to let me on the plane with that whole case unless I check it."

"Corkscrew?"

"Night stand."

I uncorked a bottle of red and got a couple of hermetically sealed glasses from the bathroom, where some hosiery hung from the shower-curtain rod. There was me looking like shit in the mirror, a big dandruff chunk suspended in my ruffled bangs. Nice one. I picked it out and flicked it into the sink. In the next room the laptop loudly announced the end of its hibernation.

"Kat, listen, I'm one quarter drunk. I take no responsibility for the shit that comes out of my mouth."

Kat said, "I've been talking to you for years in my head. I've even said precisely this to you before, except to myself."

"Look, I don't know why I lied, but I don't really have a fiancée. Well, she was at one point."

"Did you lie about the website? With the cat?"

"No, the cat's real. If you have wireless here I can show you."

Kat's compact and stylish printer began turning blank pages into remembrance. When three or four pages had gathered in the tray, she handed them to me and said, "This is the beginning."

It didn't take me long to get through them. There was the microscope incident, little embellishments like the Popsicle mold and Mr. Warner's ridiculous scolding. Kat reclined on the bed watching the Weather Channel's swirling Doppler orb of digitized blizzard. I read in the chair, my chest aching. I scanned the room quickly for a receptacle into which I could vomit if it came to that. On this thing she called a memoir were hung pieces of my recollections like little skinned animals. I wondered if I should cut through the niceties and just threaten the lawsuit right now. I never mowed the lawn of a guy named Mr. Dickman. My parents never caught me smoking, much less staged some kind of intervention with pictures of blackened lungs. She'd gotten some things right, like the mood at the end of the school year and those two wettened words she had spoken into my ear at the locker. The gentle roll of *I'm ovulating,* the potential it implied.

"You're a good writer," I said.

"I don't want to sound like a dick, but I don't need your critique. I just need to know if you're going to sic a lawyer on me."

"I don't read a lot of fiction."

"It's a *memoir*," Kat said.

"I meant I don't read much that reads like fiction. I read XML guides, medical journals. *The Wall Street Journal*."

My phone vibrated in my pocket. I extracted it and saw it was L.

"I've got to take this," I said. "Are you going to be up for awhile?"

"Is it your fake fiancée?"

"I'll be right back." I waited until the fifth ring, the last before voicemail, when I was in the hall, to press the talk button. "Gorgeous," I said, "how are you?"

"So who are you fucking in Albany?"

"I told you in my message. It's the snow. It's coming down thick and I'm stranded at some hotel by the airport. I'll try to get the first flight I can tomorrow." I rounded a corner, passing an ice machine processing cubes.

"I don't understand why you didn't go through LaGuardia or JFK."

"We got a killer deal from our travel agent. You know we're being hard-assed about keeping expenses down before profitability. Ridiculous, though, I know. I probably saved the company two hundred bucks coming this way."

"Are you in your room?" L said. I pictured her voice as a seismic green line, a sequence of pitches mapped on a monitor. In my head a team of scientists assembled around the printed output and pointed at the various peaks and

41

valleys demarcating the tone of her voice. *She's disappointed in you for leaving your message on her land line, which you both know she never picks up*, they noted.

"I was getting some ice when you called. Now I'm in my room. Did you get the package I DHL'ed from Reykjavik?"

"Yes, I tried it on. It's scratchy."

"A hundred percent Icelandic wool. It's all fish and sheep there, as far as industries go. Some aluminum, which is a controversy. Environmental whatever. The sheep have done a number on the ecosystem, overgrazed the place. There's this island off the coast with these sheer cliffs, and grass growing on top of it. The farmers take their sheep out there and hoist them to the top with rope and pulleys to graze."

"I like how it looks. It's just scratchy."

"Wear it over something. It'll come in handy at Tahoe," I said, standing in my room in front of a suitcase as messy as a crime scene.

"We're still going to Tahoe?" she said.

"I guess I can cancel the reservations for that one."

"Your presentations went okay?" she said.

"You care?"

"I own ten thousand shares in your little company, remember."

"Right, well as a shareholder you'll be happy to know it went as well as could be expected."

"Do you want to jack off?" she said.

"I—"

"You'll jack off when I tell you to jack off."

"Okay, hold on." I removed my jacket, took the phone with me to the bathroom, and leaned against the counter. "All right."

L said, "I'm in a hotel and the front desk gives me the wrong key. When I get to the room, it's already occupied. There are three black guys inside watching sports on TV, drinking beer."

I yanked my belt loose and wrestled my genitals out of my pants, lying my balls against the cool tile sink counter. My dick tried to decide whether it wanted to be hard. There were three little complimentary bottles lined up next to the mini soaps—shampoo, conditioner, moisturizing lotion—each bearing the name of a natural ingredient that likely provided no pharmacologic benefit. I noticed that the Kleenex dispenser had a sticker on it that stated it had been manufactured in Troy, New York. Well that's great. People should be proud to supply the world with easy ways to grab a tissue. I had no idea why sex was still part of what I did with L. I looked at my dick. It wasn't responding to the sexual fantasy she was breathing into the phone. I peeled the sticker off the tissue dispenser and affixed it to the head of my cock. *Made proudly in Troy, New York.* I faked my orgasm.

"Whoa," I said.

"Icelandair doesn't even fly through Albany," L said.
"Huh?"

"I thought you said you flew in to Albany from Reykjavik."

"I did," I said. "I flew in to JFK, then took this little twin-engine thing up to Albany. I know it's a messed up itinerary. That's what my admin was able to book for me."

"You're such a fucking liar," she said, her voice catching me with that intern in my office again.

"Well, I didn't even jerk off."

"Fuck you, Cedar."

"Fuck you, too, L."

Kat knocked. I hung up, got my penis back in my pants, and opened the door. Kat handed me a new stack of pages. "This is the next chapter. You'll probably not find anything libelous in here. It's all about me."

I took the pages and stared at them for a moment, three black dudes still nailing my ex-fiancée in my head.

"Am I allowed to come in?" Kat said.

"Okay."

Kat landed in the wheeled desk chair and rolled over to the window. She parted the vertical blinds and checked the snowfall. "How'd your conversation with your *fiancée* go?"

"Fine. I just lied to her about why I'm in Albany of all places. And I haven't even done anything wrong."

"That part will come," Kat said.

Oh, about twenty-two years prior, on the other side of the country, this time with Kat narrating.

My father is holding my face under water in the bathtub. My ears remain above the surface, exposed to his slurred reprimand. I have stolen a twenty-dollar bill from his wallet and this is what I get for being a thieving cunt. My nose is pressed to the bottom of the tub, along the gray streak where the enamel has been rubbed away by years of shuffling feet. The faucet infuses the warm water with a countervailing system of cold. I know I'm going to die like this and to temper the panic I repeat the word *Houdini*, over and over in my head. My mother is screaming and the hand on the back of my neck loosens enough for me to struggle up for air. My mother smashes a perfume bottle on my father's head and the room is overtaken by the smell of cheap, astringent jasmine. As I rise from the bath fully clothed and soaked, he pulls himself into the corner by the toilet, into which he vomits, passing out with one arm draped over the bowl as though confiding an intimate secret to the fixture.

My mother. Her tall willowy body is worked over by cigarette smoke that susses the premature wrinkles from her glazed Californian skin. She was a backup singer in a band from the sixties whose songs are no longer heard on the radio. The Rose Petals. There she is shimmying onstage in a couple of archival videos. She is wearing a yellow sleeveless dress and white go-go boots. Her arms pivot at the elbows like human windmills and her hair, by her account, took two hours to prepare. Now she works as a secretary at an escrow-and-title company. She was once reprimanded for wearing white lipstick to work.

We live in the eastern part of Washington state. At the back of my classroom I rub the ridge of mountains on the three-dimensional map of the United States that divides my state into brown and green, hoping that someday I'll live on the green side. The ridge reminds me of the time my mother's friend Gail let me put my finger in her baby boy's mouth. He smiled and cooed, biting down with a pair of pink, toothless, grinding mountain ranges.

And in an instant, and gradually, and inevitably, and sadly, and full of fury, and accompanied by a storm of airborne silverware, and beating the steering wheel and crying, and saying out loud she could really fucking use some dope right about now, and after checking the balance on the savings account, and wearing her nicest dress purchased from the sale rack at JCPenney's, and swearing that if she had a gun things would end in a much messier fashion, and stopping at a rest area to pee and looking again at the mesmerizing photos in her battered copy of Vincent Bugliosi's *Helter Skelter,* and singing along to Dolly Parton on the radio, and striking him in the face with a phone book, of all possible projectiles, and knowing she could really kick his ass right now because he could barely stand up *you wasted fuck,* and telling me to hurry get all my things don't bring anything stupid just what you need, and showing me the few bills in her wallet, and taking the even fewer bills from his wallet, and parking the car outside the club where she said women were paid to dance, and telling me to sit tight for a few hours with my Nancy Drew mystery, and after coming home from AA, and after coming out of the dancing place three hours later and three hundred dollars richer, and after eleven years of living with the cheap bastard whose secondary monthly expense was pull-tabs, and with her key in the ignition, my mother finally leaves my father and takes me across the mountains to the green side.

My mother gets two jobs, one as a maid at a hotel downtown, another as a waitress at a restaurant. I flatten her dollar-bill tips with a Vietnamese-English dictionary that came with our apartment, and line them up on her dresser.

My mother is a failure as a cook. When she asks me what my favorite thing is that she makes, I am being honest when I say, "TV dinners." She is a tragic baker whose cookies must be pried from the baking sheet with a butter knife. Making a marble cake is far too challenging; she simply mixes the white and chocolate powdered mixes together to avoid the trouble. Her Ore-Ida French fries have grainy, dry interiors and a freezer burned aftertaste. She makes one thing exceptionally well—asparagus quiche. When she invites men to stay over, men from AA usually, this is the dish she prepares. My understanding of asparagus is that it is only ever eaten in an eggy pie. I come to associate that funky smell of my urine with my mother's headboard banging into the wall separating our rooms. The men stay long enough for dinner, but I rarely see them at breakfast. I am an annoyance to them, something to be placated with coffee-flavored hard candies and quarters drawn magically from behind an ear. On some level I understand that the activity my mother is engaging in is sex, but I resist making a connection between the noises in the next room and the mashing together of genitals. To me it sounds like some heroic battle, like lion taming or bull fighting.

My mom makes it to AA at least twice a week. I play dolls in the church while she smokes in the basement with a cast of others who look like us, like they have some crazy story to tell involving recklessly driven cars and the early hours of the morning. That's 90 percent of the fun of AA, my mom says, hearing other people's wild-ass tales. Sometimes I sit hidden from view on the steps to the meeting space, or press my ear against a heating grate to eavesdrop. There was the man who backed over his dog in the driveway. A guy who drank lighter fluid. A woman who woke up naked on a ferris wheel.

One night a priest finds me curled up, asleep on a pew. He kneels and quietly says, *Psst*. He seems younger than any adult I know and wears glasses that make him look sort of like Buddy Holly. He says his name is Father Roth and asks if I want to see his study. I say okay and follow him to a room at the back of the church. He asks if I go to church and I tell him my mother and I only go to church for AA. He has a wind-up frog in his desk that he lets me play with and his breath smells like orange liqueur. He tells me stories from the Bible and when AA is finished tells my mother how well-behaved and smart I am.

Over several months, I spend hours playing with my second-hand, artificial-fruit-smelling Strawberry Shortcake dolls on the floor of Father Roth's study as he prepares his sermons. My mother apologizes for my bothering him but he tells her it is a pleasure to have me around. Sometimes he flicks jelly beans from his desk and I race to find them behind the furniture and in his bookcases. He tells me about a friend of his named Dennis and all the things they do together. Waterskiing, hiking in the mountains. I ask if Dennis is a priest, too. No, Father Roth laughs, Dennis owns a store that sells kitchen cabinets and sinks. He tells me that Dennis is the kindest person he has ever met, that Dennis is full of compliments and jokes. I tell Father Roth I want to meet Dennis. Oh, you can never meet Dennis, not at church anyway. I am confused. Father Roth explains that Dennis is not a member of the Catholic faith. I am perplexed. Dennis has not felt a need for Jesus in his life, Father Roth explains, but Father Roth loves him nonetheless.

I say "I thought love was for boyfriends and girlfriends." Father Roth laughs again and says that to know Jesus is to know love for all people. In fact, Father Roth says, he loves me, Kat, too.

"Me?" I say.

"Yes, you," Father Roth laughs, and picks me up to give me a hug.

Sometimes I see Father Roth at the grocery store or downtown. He always greets my mother and me warmly and has something upbeat to say. It amazes me to see him in street clothes, knowing that he is actually an undercover man of God. When I ask my mom if she would ever consider marrying Father Roth, she explains that priests never get married. Later, I ask Father Roth if he ever wants to have a wife. He shrugs and explains that the life of the priesthood suits him, that he has Jesus and his congregation and friends and that is enough.

One night at AA I find Father Roth in his study with all the lights off, weeping. When I approach him he quickly turns on a lamp and dabs his eyes with a tissue. I ask what's wrong.

Father Roth says, "Well last night I was watching *Miami Vice* and usually Dennis and I like to watch *Miami Vice* together, but this time Dennis said he wanted to stay home. So I didn't think anything of it, and watched *Miami Vice* by myself. A little while later Dennis called and said he had taken a bunch of sleeping pills and that he didn't want to live anymore. So I called 911 and rushed over to his condo and got there about the same time as the paramedics. Oh, Katie, you don't need to be hearing this."

"It's okay, I say, you can tell me."

"All right," Father Roth says, then cries some more. "So I spent last night at the hospital after they pumped his stomach and I haven't slept since. I've been praying for Dennis all day. I haven't eaten, I'm just a wreck. Oh it's awful, so awful."

"It's not your fault," I say, putting my arms around Father Roth's neck. He weeps for a full minute then holds me out at arms length.

"Oh Katie, will you do something for me? Will you do Father Roth a special favor?"

"Okay," I say.

"Okay, I am going to kneel here and confess that I am a sinner. And when I say it, could you hug me and say, I love you Father Roth? Can you do that for me? Please?"

Father Roth falls to his knees and raises his arms and his red, teary face. "Dear Lord I am a sinner!" he blubbers. Responding to my cue, I embrace him and said, "I love you, Father Roth," then step back.

"I am a sinner!"

"I love you, Father Roth."

"A sinner!"

"I love you, Father Roth!"

After the fifth time I wonder when he is going to stop. After about ten more times I start to panic. His lamentations grow more intense and harder to understand through his crying.

"I Ah a sssnnn!"

"I! Love! You! Father! Roth!"

My mother appears in the doorway and Father Roth mutters, "oh dear," and quickly rises to his feet.

"What the *fuck* is going on here?" my mother says.

"Please, ma'am, this is a church," Father Roth says.

"I don't care what the fuck this is. I put fifteen stitches in her father's head when he tried this kind of shit on her."

I say, "His friend wouldn't watch *Miami Vice* with him. He took a bunch of pills and had his stomach pumped."

In the car, my mother grabs my arms and squeezes them tightly. "Did he touch you? Did he touch your privates? Oh Katty, did he do anything naughty to you? Expose his weiner to you?"

"No," I say, "he just wanted a hug."

"You would tell me if he touched you, right? You would tell me without me having to ask. Because you know I would never never never be mad at you if you told. I would never be mad."

"I know," I say. And I do. She opens the glove compartment and rummages through road maps and cassette tapes to produce the cap to the perfume bottle she broke over my dad's head. "See this?" she says, putting it in my hand and squeezing my fingers around it into a fist. "This is to remind you what happens to wicked men who mess with little girls."

School. Long waxed-floor hallways with construction-paper art tacked to cork boards. A cracked porcelain drinking fountain with a rust stain that reminds me of dirty underpants. A sack lunch growing room temperature and yeasty smelling in a closet.

I am small for my age, which provides me the advantage of speed during recess and PE. Speed is especially important during fire drills in sixth grade. My homeroom teacher that year is a birding enthusiast named Mrs. Holmstead.

She has worked here long enough to teach some of her former students' children. She walks with a cane inscribed with Egyptian hieroglyphics, wears thick woolen suit coats and bell bottoms, drinks mint tea from an ancient mug the same putrid color as her teeth, and militantly enforces the rules of diagramming sentences. Another school building of our district burned down in 1956, a tragedy in which three children died. Mrs. Holmstead was there at the time, and takes fire drills very seriously. No one challenges her on her method. While other teachers ask that their classes exit the building in an orderly fashion and form single-file lines in the soccer field, Mrs. Holmstead, upon hearing the bell, waves her cane and yells, "Run! Run by golly! *Run for your precious young lives!*"

Soccer fields are provided so that children can ostensibly partake in games. The games I partake in on the field consist of pretending I am a horse, letting my friend Margot Henry lead me around by a jump rope and command me to sit or eat grass.

Margot at age eleven is an incipient version of the Vespa-riding lesbian she later becomes. She will be the aunt who collects snow globes and Elvis paraphernalia, wears leopard-print stretch pants and cat glasses. Her tribe will drive Volvos, maintain extensive jazz vinyl collections, eat organic, maintain a pot stash, and have a kind of magical free pass to use profanity in front of children. But in the sixth grade, she purposely wears sweatshirts inside out, has the

Ryan Boudinot

most elaborate sticker book of anyone I know, and is friends with the boys who would rather play with the girls than with the sporty boys. We trade friendship pins and stick them to the laces of our shoes. We choreograph bedroom musicals to Hall and Oates songs.

"I want to show you something in my brother's bedroom," Margot says one afternoon after school. Her brother is named Neil and he floats stoned through the impossibly mature realm of high school. He isn't home when we get to Margot's house and neither are her parents. Entering Neil's room is like stepping into the temple of a foreign and terrifying religion. KISS posters decorate most of the walls, and covering the inside of the door is a poster of a gigantic hand with an upraised middle finger. As we roll on the floor laughing at the poster, we hear Neil's station wagon pull up outside. Margot grabs my hand and pulls me into Neil's closet where we crouch in a pile of smoke-smelling clothing and empty beer bottles. We hear the front door, laughter, then Neil talking to somebody. Through a crack in the closet door we see Neil and his girlfriend, a stringy-haired girl named Tia who wears the coolest embroidered jeans I have ever seen.

"We don't have much time," Neil says. "They'll be home in half an hour."

"What about your sister?"

"She's probably off playing dolls somewhere. Fuck, my cock's already so hard."

Misconception

We watch the teenagers quickly undress like it's no big deal, this otherworldly comfort they share with each other's hairy bodies. So *that's* what a boner looks like. Tia climbs on the bed and Neil moves toward her head. Something slippery sounding is happening that we can't quite see. After a few minutes of this, Neil fiddles with something he retrieves from under his mattress, then climbs between Tia's legs. There are four or five minutes of humorous butt movement. Then Neil releases a loud grunt and Tia frowns, pulls him closer, ruffles his hair. The gesture sticks in my head for years, lodged in memory as something that perhaps I will one day understand. Finding myself beneath men years later I remember the gesture and recognize it as belonging to the carnal repertoire of the disappointed, the resigned pantomime of an uneventful fuck. Neil kisses his girlfriend and says, "So how many times did you come?"

The socially collaborative mating rituals of junior high school. The careful deployment of friends to spread word of your crushes. Angry reprisals on behalf of a friend wronged. I purposely tell Margot to keep my crush on Peter Berring a secret and she faithfully alerts Peter's best friend Ben. A rendezvous is arranged behind the playground rope wall after sixth period. Peter shows up slouchy, sleepy after a day of hitting his inhaler too much, wearing a Ratt T-shirt. A small contingent of fourth graders sit eagerly on the log benches, anxious to see if we'll really go through with it. We try to shoo them away but they won't budge. We only have about ten minutes before the buses leave, it's either kiss in public or not at all. Peter and I press the squishy, wet parts of our faces together. One of the kids exclaims, scandalized at the sight of tongues.

Over the phone, Margot and I collaborate on our concept of boys, as if we are responsible for inventing them. What they would do to us, what we would do to them, what we would do together. Margot reads aloud to me from her parents' *The Joy of Sex* and when I'm at her house we study the illustrations of the hirsute couple as if we're deciphering a strange set of technical instructions on how to put together an end table, how to construct a bird house.

Cedar Rivers is a boy in my class who we call the Mad Scientist. The nickname grows from his reputation for acing science tests, but it also fits his tendency to apparently cut his mind free from whatever curricula is being hashed out on the blackboard and drift through the window into constructs Margot and I have little patience to care about. If he were decorated with acne or doughy or slack-jawed, he would join the small group of nerds who recite *Dr. Who* dialogue to each other in the back of class— guys destined to become fuckable and fabulously wealthy in software decades later. Margot and I watch Cedar play left wing in soccer and occasionally he seems to forget there's a game going on, so we yell at him to wake up. I ask Cedar for help on my science report, flick wadded pieces of paper at him in algebra class, even walk up to him on one of Margot's dares and tell him I'm ovulating. None of this appears to impress him.

One morning Cedar brings a sample of his own semen to examine under a microscope in science class. Most of the other kids bring muddy water, rotten leaves, or dead insects. After the initial excitement of looking at undulating blobs wears off, word spreads that there is something especially interesting happening at Cedar's work station. I peer into the microscope, squinting, focusing, and see hundreds of backlit, dead spermatozoa. I cannot summon the imagination required to connect a *Joy of Sex* act to the production of these cells. When I look up from the instrument Cedar wears an expression of dreadful expectation.

"Sick," I say.

As soon as our teacher Mrs. Wheeler discovers what Cedar has brought to class, she banishes him to the principal's office. I concur with the other girls in the restroom that Cedar has revolted us with his perverted, grody-to-the-max transgression. But when nobody is looking, I return to the science room to take the slide from the microscope and slip it into my pencil case.

My mother brings home Ed, the truck driver who tells me that three billion Chinese can't be wrong about acupuncture. She brings home Russell, who breeds dogs. Barry, a keyboard player in a cover band. Sam, who's missing a finger. Three guys named Matt in a row. These auditions seem to come to an end with George, who is tall and old and has the word *manager* in his job title. He tells me he has a daughter of his own, nine years older than me, who lives in California. He shows me pictures he has in his wallet, of them sledding together, bundled on an overcast morning at a ski resort, arms thrown out in defiance of aerodynamics. There's a picture of Anne, that's her name—as in *of Green Gables,* as in Frank—playing flute in a marching band. Anne's first communion. Anne's studio portrait from Olan Mills, in which she's wearing the most hellish fuchsia velour I have ever seen. George drinks and compliments my mother's coffee as we sit at the dining-nook table. He shows me a picture of Anne dressed as a ballerina and tells me it was from Halloween. I watch the veins in George's hands roll around like night crawlers underneath his skin as he reaches for a carton of milk. Later, my mother makes him asparagus quiche but I do not hear the corresponding smack of the headboard. Strangely, this delights my mother.

George pulls into the driveway in a rented RV and announces he's taking us on a trip across the mountains. I hide in my bedroom until my mother extracts me with a combination of threats and promises. I brace myself for a return to the brown part of the state.

The RV smells of mildew and Pine-Sol and bears signs of the retired couple who own it. George calls them the Coopers, and in the framed photo on the wall of the bathroom they have caught a large bass and are holding it proudly between them. Mostly I sit at the back table by the window, eating Whoppers from a paper cup, watching droplets of rain bloat as they slide past the plastic fish-eye lens adhered to the window to enhance the range of the rear-view mirror up front. George and my mother sing Burt Bacharach songs in the cab of the vehicle, my mother's practiced soprano curled protectively around George's tone-deaf growl. First I let the chocolate layer of the Whopper dissolve in my mouth, then enjoy the structural breakdown of the malt ball, a disintegrating, petrified foam. My period makes an appearance in my panties. One gas station and a wrecked pair of jeans later, we're back on the road, George making pronouncements from the driver's seat that I have nothing to be embarrassed about, that God made women a certain way, like with really deluxe plumbing, and even if it seems gross it's all according to His plan. My mother slips me two of her Tylenols with codeine she bought in bulk in Canada.

We pull off the road somewhere on the eastern side of the pass, the RV tilting a bit to the passenger side as we come to a halt. I let a lone Whopper roll off the Formica table onto the floor. George curses under his breath. A semi roars past, its wake of air rocking our vehicle. A deck of cards on the side table slides against the wall. Bottles jostle one another in the pantry. My mother holds onto the wall as she climbs from the cab and makes her way back toward me.

"Something's wrong with the engine," she says.

George gets out. With a great creaking the trailer lurches starboard. This time bottles and boxes of cereal fly out of the pantry. The bathroom door opens and smacks my mother in the forehead. All remaining Whoppers quickly migrate off the table. I can't hear what George is saying over our screaming, but I know it's something about getting out. I climb over containers of food, paperbacks, cassette tapes, and bottles of soda, following my mom to the cab. We're almost sideways. The door to the residence portion of the RV is facing down. Fir boughs obscure the right-side window. Mom's legs disappear out through the open driver's-side window. As I crawl to the front, the RV slowly tilts even more. George's sweaty face pokes in, yells at me to hurry up. I make it to the cab. He circles my wrists with his hands and, in what seems like a single motion, yanks me out. It takes me a minute to understand what has happened to the vehicle. George has pulled over onto a soft gravel shoulder on an embankment, which is quickly starting to erode under the vehicle's weight. The RV leans against two young fir trees, the only things preventing it from tumbling into a ravine. As the three of us stand perplexed and shaken, a truck pulls up. A Burt Reynolds–looking logger joins us to assess the situation.

"That's one hell of a tow job you got there," the logger says.

I suppose so, George says. The saplings snap, and with a great crashing rumble our rented vehicle of recreation tumbles side over side through the trees, flinging our belongings from the windows and flapping doors, finally coming to rest upside down some fifty feet below.

The logger takes off his hat and wipes his brow. "Not exactly a tow job anymore," he says.

Of course our vacation is now ruined, with George and my mother not speaking, and me sitting between them in the logger's expansive front seat as he drives us to the next big town, where we'll rent a car. The plan is to return to the scene, pick through the wreckage for our things, and wait for a towing crew. While George fills out the paperwork for the car, my mom and I find ourselves alone in a gas station restroom. She gives me a look, an *oh shit, what did we get into?* I return it, and we both laugh, a little at first, then bent over double, holding onto the sink for support. Suddenly this is the best vacation I can remember. In the rented Toyota on our way back to the scene, George sucks air through his teeth and mutters about insurance premiums. My mother and I communicate via a language of raised and lowered eyebrows. The game is to make the other laugh, but as soon as one of us does, George bellows that there's nothing damn funny about this, that we're going to have a hell of a time gathering our stuff, and that the Coopers are not going to be pleased about what happened to their vacation transportation and winter home.

At the ravine, we scramble down the embankment, picking up items of clothing and scattered toiletries. I find my mother's hair dryer, smashed to pieces on a rock. Inside the RV there is a mess of food, bedding, utensils, and cleaning products. George crawls over the rocks and weeds holding objects aloft and asking whether they belong to us or the Coopers. He wants to put them in two distinct piles. He becomes upset that he's lost his silver grooming set, which includes a toenail clipper, nail file, tweezers, and an engraved toothpick.

"I can't lose my kit," George says. "My dad gave it to me when I graduated from high school. Are these socks yours?"

The mountains around us soon threaten to hide us in twilight and George and my mom loudly debate whether to drive home in the rental car. The tow truck George called is nowhere to be seen. I find the grooming kit under a road atlas inside the upside-down RV and pocket it without telling George. He sits on a fallen log numbly eating graham crackers squirted with fake cheese from a can, occasionally making pronouncements about substandard highway construction.

We try to bargain with the daylight, hold out for as long as we can before admitting it is night, then resign ourselves to the fact that we'll be spending the night here. My mom probes the inside of the RV with a flashlight, arranging cushions and blow-up mattresses on what used to be the ceiling. I crawl inside a sleeping bag and nest in a corner in the back, a table suspended above my head. George and mom settle into a place next to the bathroom. When they start snoring I escape by crawling through the window, dragging the sleeping bag behind me. When I get to the rental car, I throw George's grooming set as far as I can into the deep woods.

Albany again.

"*Cool,*" I said. "You said *cool* when you looked at my slide in the microscope."

Kat snored in the chair. I still had a handful of pages to go. I skimmed ahead. Kat developed a crush on me, after a series of other boyfriends. Dry humping in Paul's garage, holding hands at the mall, the microscope, menstruation, the trading of slides. And this: *It ribbons out of the tiny portal at the tip, a white slo-mo stream like windblown hair in a commercial for shampoo, hanging for a moment, propelled upward until gravity lies it on the back of my hand in a pattern suggesting a treble clef.* I read the passage a second time, unable to recall the experience. I thought I'd experienced my first orgasm with a girl two years later: Paige Phillips, the eyeliner addict. This was some part about Kat making me come with a combo blow/hand job in George's van, parked in the driveway.

"Finished?" Kat said, waking into a stretch.

"I don't remember this thing with, uh, you and me in the van."

"It might not have happened exactly like that. It felt right, structurally."

"I thought this was a memoir."

"Maybe it happened with another boy, but I thought it would be good to include."

"You said *cool* when you looked into the microscope, not *sick*. It wasn't Mrs. Holmstead who had the freaky thing about fire drills, it was Mrs. Holland."

"Mrs. *Holland*. That's right. I'll change that." Kat stretched out of the chair. "Look, Cedar, it's not like I'm consulting an almanac to write this thing. All I need from you is to tell me if there's anything in there you want me to cut so that I don't find myself in court."

"You want me to just read your memoir, half of it written from my point of view, and rubber stamp it? That's why we're here?"

Kat pinched the bridge of her nose. "It's just legal shit my editor gave me."

"Can we set aside the legal shit? I'm not going to sue you. I'll keep reading. I promise I won't nitpick. You're right. Who cares about the name of our teacher? Let me see the rest."

"I have to go print it. And I did say *sick,* not *cool.*"

Kat left. I settled into the chair she had occupied, into the warmth of her body retained by the upholstery, and stared at the leatherette booklet containing the motel's phone numbers and amenities. The Weather Channel played the storm. I considered going to Kat's room and asking for the entire manuscript, but cautioned myself. She was doling it out a section at a time as if through a series of safety valves.

What it boiled down to was this: as long as I didn't fuck Kat, I still had a chance to patch it together with L. One fuck in an office with a twenty-two-year-old intern was a mistake, two fucks was a habit. I was going to have to not fuck Kat.

I Googled *Kat Daniels,* pulling up 347 results, the first few of which were about a porn star. I clicked a couple links and determined this wasn't the same Kat Daniels. I flipped to the title page of Kat's memoir. *Katherine* Daniels. I found her book, *Nymphonomicon,* on Amazon and read the review:

Katherine Daniels's short stories, collected in *Nymphonomicon,* introduce the radical aesthetics of early nineties riot-grrrl feminism to the otherworldliness of postwar European fiction in the vein of Danilo Kis or Bohumil Hrabal. She appears to have digested Angela Carter's oeuvre and Bataille's *Story of the Eye,* using their perverse energies to limn the dirty secrets of her generation. In "Oranges," a woman keeps her boyfriend in a lunch box, while the title story is a woman's sexual history told in the form of entries in the yellow pages. "The Weight of Blood" employs an unnamed city's S-M subculture as a strangely affecting milieu in which to expose a man's childhood traumas involving a pinewood derby. At turns affectionate and bitingly perverse, Daniels pulls the reader through the more convoluted recesses of the human psyche while rendering physical, human contact electrically real on the page.

—*Ryan Boudinot*

Whatever that means. The handful of customer reviews were split between five stars and one. The cover image, a reproduction of some grainy vintage erotica with the title and author name placed strategically over the nipples and pubic area looked intriguing enough. I signed in and ordered it.

Kat returned with the next batch of pages.

"I ordered your book," I said.

"I would've given you one for free. I have a few copies with me."

"I Googled you. You're a porn star."

"Different Kat Daniels. She's got way bigger tits than me."

"My first cadaver dissection was a woman with implants. Have you ever seen a cadaver?"

"I can't say I have."

"They're fascinating," I said. "Out of everything in med school, cadaver lab was my favorite."

"I guess that shouldn't surprise me."

"You get to see parts of bodies that the bodies themselves never saw."

"Like a memoir. You get to see parts of lives that those living them never saw."

I glanced at the clock and thought I should get on with the next chapter, but I was enjoying Kat's company. It was like the college experience of having a girlfriend, staying up in waves of mock profound logorrhea, suggesting a two-in-the-morning recon to a mini-mart for unhealthy food, smoking bad hash from a crunched soda can. That period, when I would have most enjoyed getting to know Kat, when both of us were most interesting and consumed with unrealistic plans, was a comatose pause between us. Our initial, pubescent compatibility had degraded. Now we were old, with histories tied up in other people. This flavor of strangeness, this witnessing of the momentum of another person's ripening and the onslaught of decay, was precisely the reason why I wanted desperately, suddenly, to put my cock in any place she offered. Just to see what it was like, to extract eroticism from sheer weirdness. Instead, I continued to read her book.

Cedar recounting some
events from back
in the day.

One afternoon that summer Kat called sounding panicked and asked me to meet her at Burger King. I rode my bike across town and found her in a booth drinking a shake, using a spork to move piles of salt around on a placemat.

"Last night my dad called," she said. "He wants to meet me across the street at Kentucky Fried Chicken in half an hour. I don't want to see him by myself."

"Does your mom know he's here?"

Kat shook her head. "I wouldn't be seeing him if she did."

We spotted Kat's father's van—a white beaten-up Ford with the name of his employer, Apex Septic, stenciled crappily on the side—across the street in the KFC parking lot. A man appeared to be sleeping inside. The tailgate bore an ideology in the form of a bumper sticker: *Bosses are like diapers. Full of shit and always on your ass!!!* We crossed the street. Kat went to the driver's side and stood looking at him awhile. He must have realized he was being watched and, startled, he jerked his head, smiled, and adjusted his baseball cap.

"Katie Lady! I'm so happy to see you!" the man said, hugging his daughter in the parking lot. "You hungry? Who's your friend?"

"I'm Cedar."

"As in the tree? Cool name, dude. I'm Jerry. You guys in the mood for some extra crispy?"

As we went inside, Kat whispered to me to stand in line with Jerry while she went to the restroom.

"You Kat's boyfriend?" he said.

"Yeah, I guess so."

"Cool. I always wondered when she'd start seeing boys. You going out for any sports?"

"I'll probably do tennis next year."

"No football? You look like you could be a wide receiver. What's wrong witchoo man? Don't worry, I'm shitting you. You got a favorite flavor? I'm kind of partial to original style."

"I like barbecue."

"Yeah, barbecue's great. And we'll have to get biscuits and gravy, too. Coleslaw. Whatever you want, man, let me know. My treat."

We ordered and found a booth. "You a big movie fan?" Jerry said.

"Sure."

"Ever see *War Games*?"

"Yeah."

"Want. To. Play. A. Game? Ha. Yeah, all that crazy shit. I was an extra in that motherfucker. I'm not shitting you. Shot those military base scenes up in the mountains in an old mining camp. Put me in a soldier uniform and had me chase after a truck waving a fake M-16 all day. Those Hollywood fuckers do boatloads of coke. Sound guy invited me into his trailer and let me do a few lines. But I don't do that kind of shit anymore. I'm completely straight, have been for some time now, a year and three months. Back then, though, that was a different story. One of the makeup chicks, man, we got to talking and before you know it I was asking her if I could see her with her knees behind her ears, you know what I'm talking about. Here comes Katie. Sweetheart!"

Kat slid into the booth beside me as our order arrived.

Jerry said, "I got apples in my truck for you, just picked yesterday. I've been doing some extra work at an orchard. I have this arrangement with the bossman there to fix equipment. They let me take home all the apples I want. Nice ones, too, the ones they send to Japan. All the crummy apples they turn into cider. You guys have jobs this summer?"

"I babysit sometimes," Kat said.

"I mow lawns."

"Good, good," Jerry said. "What are you guys holding back for, dig in! There's way more chicken here than I'll ever eat. So you're going to be in high school next year?"

Kat nodded.

"You promise to study hard?"

"Yeah."

"That's one of my biggest regrets, you know," Jerry said, screwing his hat tighter onto his head by the bill. "If I would of taken it a little more serious at the time, that's all I'm saying. But you're smart, way smarter than I ever was. You'll do good in high school."

"Why did you want to meet me here?" Kat said.

"I thought you liked fried chicken."

"I mean why did you want to meet me at all."

Jerry took off his hat, bent the bill, and put it back on again. "Hey. Okay, I see where you're coming from. I got you. I know it's weird, me calling you up out of the blue and all that. I was going to be in the area anyway, and I just thought it would be good to see you. To catch up on things."

"I haven't seen you in like years or something."

Jerry turned to me, laughed nervously. "See, man, she's mad at me. And you know what? She has every reason in the world to be."

Beneath the table Kat locked her fingers around mine. "I'm not mad at you," she said, "I just don't understand why you wanted to meet now."

He sighed. "Because I wanted to apologize. You know how things work with AA. I've been going for the last few years, like, you know, I should of always done. And one of the big deals for AA is apologizing to people you hurt in the past. I don't expect you to like me or anything, I know I did some fucked up stuff—"

"You broke my arm," Kat said.

"It was an accident, Katty. I . . . Yeah, like okay, breaking your arm. Which I didn't mean to do at all. But what a shit thing to do, yeah. I know a bunch of words from an ex-drunk are worth nothing, I know that. And I know there'll always be part of you which hates me. I accept your hate as part of my punishment. There's all this talk of higher powers and stuff in AA. I've been thinking a lot about repentance, like what it's supposed to be about. My folks never were big into church, and I never saw much use in it. Until recently, anyway. Few weeks ago I went to this wetback Catholic church, right? Because it was close to my house and I saw on TV how they have these booths you can sit in and confess shit to the priest. So I went there and went into one of the booths, but there was no priest on the other side, so I figured you had to stay in there until the priest came. I got scared that if I left I'd fuck up my chance to repent. So, yeah, I wasn't really thinking straight. I ended up hanging out in that booth overnight, falling asleep in there. Later I realized they had hours of confession posted outside, but they were in Spanish, so same difference. The priest found me the next morning and asked if I wished to confess. I said yeah, and he said he didn't take confession until after he had his morning coffee. So we went back to his little office where they keep the supplies, the community wafers and wine and stuff, and I ended up telling him everything there that I would have told him in the booth anyway. Old Mexican dude, named Father Jimenez. Studied in a seminary in Colombia, turns out. The sad part to me came when I realized I couldn't even remember some of the bad shit I'd done, probably couldn't remember the worst shit, and the worst shit I ever done was the shit I did to you. So I'm there with Father Jimenez crying my guts out, telling him all this stuff and I like start to become more aware of what it is I'm actually doing. Like I see myself from outside of my own body. And the fucked-up thing I think is that this confession stuff, it doesn't erase the original deed. And in a way, it's like you can fuck up all you want, and then you wipe the slate clean with a confession. Those Catholics, man, they have it figured out. Go ahead and fuck up, just make sure to confess.

"Which, to me, seems really fucked up, wouldn't you say? So I leave the church after about a box and a half of Kleenex, and I go out to my truck and sit there for about an hour. Listen to a rock station playing wall-to-wall Meat Loaf with no commercial interruptions. And I fucking hate Meat Loaf, but I made myself listen to that shit sort of as punishment. I start thinking about how to confess and have it actually mean something. What I came up with was this: when you do something wrong, and realize what you did was wrong, a true confession is a way to understand the wrongness of your action the deepest way you can. It's not going to fix whatever it is you did, the damage is done, but it's a way to tell yourself not to fuck up again. Because all you can really accomplish is to become a little better so you don't fuck up so bad next time."

Jerry pulled his straw in and out of its lid, making a sound like an out-of-tune violin. He trembled a moment, trying to cough out some words. "That's why I'm here, to confess to you that I hurt you and was mean to you and that I live with my own self-hatred for it. And this apology is my way to tell you that I want to understand what it must have felt like for you. I know I'll never reach the same level of hurt you felt, but I'll never stop trying to put myself in your shoes and will never forgive myself for it. Even if you forgive me totally, I won't let go of this anger at myself. I know I can't offer you guys much. I'm just a fucking septic-tank pumper who lives in Bumfuck, Egypt, with a van and a three-room shack and a shop. But I want you to know that I would drop anything if you need me, that I will go after anyone who hurts you. I just want to say that I love you, Katie."

We were suspended in a coldness.

"Are you finished?" Kat said.

Misconception

"I . . ."

"I've heard enough of what you have to say. Let's go, Cedar."

What Jerry did next was *slump*, though the word implies this was merely a physical gesture. He had expected this response and knew he didn't deserve any better. Yet still he had hoped. His sorrow pulled his eyes down toward his hands, folded over a piece of greasy chicken growing cold. Pathetically, he took a pencil from his shirt pocket and slowly filled in a three-letter word on a crossword puzzle printed on his placemat. Shaking, I followed Kat out. She crossed the street to Burger King and went behind the building.

"He broke your arm? You never told me that. What happened?"

"I can't."

We were surrounded by the smell of scorched meat. Semis barreled by on the freeway. Kat asked me to watch for Jerry's van and let her know when it was gone. I peered around the corner and saw Jerry climb slowly back into his vehicle. He sat with his hands on the steering wheel and slowly let his head sag forward until it rested against the soiled sheepskin cover. I watched him cry but couldn't hear him. I heard Kat crying but was afraid to look at her.

As Kat's Alaskan voyage approached, summer grew dense with its anxieties. Dusk, in bed, I listened to my parents' muffled, pained conversation through the wall, my mother's voice a warble of concern, my father's cagy and evasive, while I absentmindedly felt myself through my pajamas. They were arguing something fierce. Something about my dad being disbarred. Something about a client. Mother-made noises on the precipice of tears, a sworn word. As far as I could tell, the culture of the courtroom inspired only nausea for my father anymore. He'd had a string of bad cases, each loss compounding his fear that his own shortcomings, not justice, were to blame. He admitted that he arrived at court ill-prepared, delivered his arguments poorly, blew openings in cross-examination, hesitated to raise objections, suffered from bowel-churning prehearing anxiety. The judges were sanctimonious pricks, prosecutors appeared gleeful when they saw him on defense, and the criminals he represented were ungrateful and deserving of sentences far harsher than they received. He'd quit the whole thing, he said, turn his back on the catastrophe of his career and raise llamas. As they argued, the correlation presented itself more acutely: my father and the very idea of justice were both failures.

I didn't want to end up like my dad. I needed a plan. Days later, at dinner, I announced that I would throw myself into my schoolwork the following year and get the grades necessary for admission to an Ivy League university. I translated their masticating grunts to mean they'd believe it when they saw it, or maybe they were reacting not to what I'd said, but merely to the fact I had spoken.

My mother, meanwhile, was enjoying a sort of career renaissance. She'd been contacted by a notable publisher who wanted to use some of her photos in a new physiology text. One night, while studying her hematoma series, I asked her why anatomy and physiology were separate areas of study, why they weren't combined. She explained that anatomy was about forms, connections, components. Physiology, concerning the functions of these forms, existed *within* anatomy. More granular still were histology, biochemistry, and molecular biology, each subject cradled within the others until human knowledge ultimately yielded to the mysteries of subatomic particles. You could look at individual human beings as if through a microscope, she explained, adjusting the magnification to capture the whole body, the pumping heart, a cell within the heart, an organelle within the cell, a molecule within the organelle.

That night, in the fuzzy-edged haze after masturbation, I adjusted this theoretical microscope in the other direction, thinking about bodies as members of families, cultures, races, species. Psychology, sociology, anthropology. Here was the plane on which my father struggled, wrestling meaning and consequence from the troubles these bodies put themselves in. In bed, with cold spunk pooling in my belly button, I consciously witnessed my brain opening its awareness more fully to the world. I thought about the years ahead of me as if they were laid out in a gigantic calendar with squares of days teeming with life, cities, sex, flocks of birds, knowledge. I became aware that I was maturing, as freighted as the word was with uninspired, health-class baggage. I needed a long-term plan. I cleaned up with a tissue and walked from my room through the house to my mother's study. Books lined most of one wall, reference volumes and textbooks, neural science, organic chemistry, orthopedic physical assessment, pathology, pharmacology. If I began now, I'd have a head start for medical school. I looked for all the textbooks that had the word *introduction* in the title and carried them back to my room. There began my teenage preoccupation with my mother's medical library, getting comfortable with my inability to comprehend most of it, savoring the reward of occasional understanding. I was determined to be a doctor. I was going to save lives.

I counted the days until Kat's month-long boat trip on one hand. When either of us broached the subject, the conversation turned to enumerating George's faults and hypocrisies, and together we developed his malignant caricature. She described a daydream in which George's house, five minutes from her own, unmoored itself from its foundation and crawled through the intervening neighborhoods leaving a swath of smashed cars, flattened house pets, and uprooted landscaping. Kat imagined opening her door and finding George's house sitting in their front yard, its peeling siding heaving from the effort. She showed me a drawing from her notebook, in which his house was mounting hers, while a terrified-looking Kat peered from her bedroom window.

I said good-bye to Kat at the pier at dawn. George and Veronica finished loading the boat and chuckled to each other at the melodrama of our tearful farewell. I watched the hot pink sky swallow them with its horizon. I pedaled home and found my house overcome with the flamboyance of scotch broom, blooming in the ditch by our side yard. My father never failed to point out that this plant was a weed, but my mom liked it, and put cuttings of it on the dining room table when it bloomed. I fused these objects of memory together into a sort of collage: sailboat, scotch broom, pink sky. I went to my bedroom and commenced a month-long memory lapse. I imagine I mowed lawns, watched movies and TV, went to the mall and the park, hung out with Paul, threw away my cigarettes, ate dinner, rode my bike, listened to my Walkman, but I don't remember any of it.

The month passed and Kat called, her voice nasal with a cold. She said something blunt and unenthusiastic like, "I'm back," then doled out little dribbles of answers as I asked about different parts of the trip. "By the way," she said, "George proposed to my mom."

The next day at Kat's house her mother was already in the process of packing their belongings to move to George's house. They needed to get out before the end of August to avoid another month's rent. Kat sat in her room, skin peeling on an eroded tan, systematically pulling elastic fibers from a sock.

"How was the trip?" I said.

"Fine. We sailed."

"How far did you get?"

"Port Hardy."

"What was it like?"

"Boring."

"What's wrong?"

"Nothing."

I attributed her mood to the engagement, or to my new unified theory of female moods: menses. Over the next week Kat refused to call me. I had to call her if I wanted to talk. We went to a movie and she made some un-enthused attempts at making out with me, but I could tell she wasn't into it. We walked to my house along the train tracks, past our old school. She wrestled her hand out of mine, annoyed. My default question was to ask what was wrong, every ten minutes or so. We devolved into a fight over something ridiculous and she turned around and walked back to her place.

Later that night she broke her phone embargo, whispering over the line. She said her period was late.

"What's that mean?" I said.

"You're the medical guy. Look it up in one of your stupid books," she said, then hung up.

I quickly consulted *Introduction to Human Reproductivity, 3rd ed.,* and discovered that Kat may have had any number of disorders, was training for a triathalon, or was pregnant. I called her back.

"How late is it? Sometimes you can miss a period and it's no big deal, it just happens. Like it happens to women who exercise a lot. Have you ever missed a period before? When was it supposed to be? Do you know when you ovulated?"

A door squeaked open in the background. Behind Kat's breathing, George said, "If you're gonna use my phone, you're going to have to obey some guidelines. No calls after nine PM, little miss."

"This isn't even your phone," Kat said.

"Well it's about to be."

Kat's voice wavered. "I have to go."

My room, a ten-by-twelve space containing the shit of my life, appeared to contract and expand with my breath. I crawled onto my bed and stared at the blobby patterns of painted-over, texturizing spackle on the wall, trying to find geographies in it. This blob looked a little like Africa. Pregnant? I wanted to do something physical, go ride my bike, mow a lawn, but segments of time had begun to compound one another, steadily gaining mass, pinning me to my bed. My mom appeared in the doorway after the perfunctory knock.

"Hey buddy, we have ice cream. Want some?"

"No."

"What's the matter?"

"Why do you always think something's wrong?"

"You're lying in your bed fully clothed with your nose against the wall."

I didn't say anything.

"It's Neapolitan. We saved the strawberry stripe for you."

"I said I didn't want any."

My mother sat down on the edge of my bed and stroked my foot.

"Knock it off," I said.

"Your parents are about the last people on earth you want to spend time with," said my mom. "Trust me, I know. I've been there. I just want you to be able to talk to us about whatever's on your mind."

"Kat broke up with me," I said without thinking. Brilliant. Now if they heard me crying in my room they'd assume it was for typical adolescent reasons.

"Oh no. I'm sorry, Cedar. That's rough. It really is," she said, then added, "The ice cream is in the freezer when you want it, okay sweetie?"

I started crying as soon as my mother left, but not because of what had happened to Kat. I hadn't begun to grasp the borders of that enormous and terrifying fact. I cried because I wanted my mom to hold me and press my face into her gaudy bead necklace. I couldn't trust my parents to guide me through this, but I couldn't remember a time when I'd needed them more.

I recreated every sexual event Kat and I had shared and tried to recall even a droplet of semen getting near her. I'd never penetrated her or even ejaculated in her presence. The blow jobs had been pantomimes of sexual pleasure in which I'd lied and said it was possible for a guy to come without anything coming out. I had yet to figure out how sex was even really supposed to feel. So there was no way it was me. It had to be someone else. Was it George? I played with this idea for a while, sort of examined it from a distance like I was holding a blob of toxic goo in front of me on a stick. If I called Kat to ask if this was the case, George might answer. A dark canyon of hatred split me down the middle. And yet I worried I was being overly dramatic. How was I supposed to behave with Kat now? What encouraging dialogue was I supposed to deliver to fulfill my role as a supportive boyfriend? What if Kat decided to keep the baby and I entered my freshman year of high school with everyone thinking I was a dad? I played another scenario, some kind of sad, bargain-basement wedding with a white sheet cake from Safeway and somebody from Kat's church playing a piano. Paul as best man, ludicrous. Quitting school to get a job. Eventually becoming the manager of a chain store at the mall. Maybe they could do some kind of DNA test to show that the baby wasn't mine. Fuck, Kat was about to go live with George. Was she planning to tell her mom? I vomited that night's fried chicken dinner into my wastebasket, hacking to encourage its passage from my throat.

The next morning, fog and spider webs covered the neighborhood. I called Kat on a gas station pay phone and arranged to meet her that afternoon at the mall food court. We sat in the most secluded booth we could find, next to a gigantic pot full of plastic plants.

"He did it, didn't he?" I said.

"Who?" Kat said, staring at the entrance of the arcade.

"It was just you three on the boat, right? You didn't meet anyone else on the way?"

"No."

"Then it must be George."

"I don't want to talk about it."

"What are you going to do? Have you taken one of those tests?"

"No."

"Don't you think you should?"

"I guess."

"What if you really are pregnant? What are you going to do?"

"I don't know."

I delivered a line from TV, "Kat, *It's not your fault.*"

"Whatever, Cedar."

"I'm trying to help. I don't know what I'm supposed to do in this situation."

"Maybe I actually should get one of those tests. Will you get it for me?" Kat pulled herself open a tiny bit and showed me something frightened, then quickly closed up again. I dragged a cold French fry through a patch of ketchup.

Later, we rode our bikes to a Texaco station mini-mart. Kat hung out by the air and water and agreed to ring the bell on her bike three times if she saw someone we knew. The birth control devices and pregnancy tests were kept behind the counter, alongside the pornography and cigarettes, a logical grouping of products. I didn't want to seem like I just wanted to buy the pregnancy test, so I put a pack of Big Red on the counter. The Hispanic guy at the register rang it up.

"And I'd like a pregnancy test, too, please."

"Sure thing, boss. What kind you want?"

"Whichever one is cheapest. And can I have that in a bag?"

"No problem, boss. You take care now."

Outside I got back on my bike. As we pedaled away from the station I hit a patch of oil and my bike skidded out from under me and slammed into the ice cooler. The pregnancy test and the Big Red went flying. Kat helped pull me up.

"You got it really bad on your elbow," she gasped. I took a look and thought I saw bone. Woozy, I leaned against the side of the building while Kat found some paper towels. The cashier had witnessed the whole thing and came out to ask if I was okay. I waved him off like it was no big deal. Meanwhile, a truck pulled up to the pump and ran over the pregnancy test.

"Oh, man," the cashier said, "I'd give you a free 'nother one but my boss gets pissed off if inventory doesn't match up."

"Do you have any money?" I asked Kat.

She opened her purse, extracted a couple bills, and handed them over.

We agreed that revealing the results of the test over the phone was too risky. We'd meet at the swings at our old school the following morning and she'd tell me personally. That night a summer storm rolled over town and the next morning it was still raining hard. Drenched, I rode my bike to the playground and huddled inside a half-buried tractor tire to stay out of the rain. Some kid had been here recently, and left a pile of grapes in the gravel. I made sure my bike was in view so Kat would know I was here, but after an hour she still hadn't showed up. I considered waiting the whole day, and pictured myself shivering, peering out the tight, sphincter-like opening of my hooded sweatshirt. I lasted another fifteen minutes. I rode half an hour to Kat's house and found the driveway empty. A few knocks on the door convinced me the place was empty. I took the front door key from under a decorative fake rock and went inside.

There were cardboard boxes stacked in the front hall and in the living room were piles of pathetic-looking bric-a-brac. The kitchen was an even bigger mess. I grabbed a stray granola bar and surveyed the fridge, its sorrowful museum of condiments. I picked up an envelope of photos and rifled through them. The Alaska vacation fanned out in swaths of green and blue. Lots of George smiling in sunglasses and a floppy hat, Windbreaker, cargo shorts, and athletic socks. Every shot of George and Veronica with their arms around each other was headless; I smiled realizing this was Kat's private revenge. There was one picture of the three of them standing on a dock, all of them beaming. It surprised me to see Kat looking so happy. In another picture Kat was reading a book in the cabin, then listening to her Walkman, then asleep with a shaft of sun falling across her face. I stashed this one in my pocket. I stared hard at a picture of George, trying to summon the loathing I knew I was supposed to feel. *He fucked her*. I whispered the words slowly, "He . . . fucked

. . . her . . ." to see if I could get any closer to what they meant.

Upstairs, I looked into the bathroom trash for any trace of the pregnancy test, but found only a wadded piece of toilet paper, a Band-Aid wrapper, a Q-tip globbed with ear wax. Kat's room was trashed, posters torn down, clothes and plastic jewelry strewn; I couldn't tell whether this was the result of moving, a tantrum, or maybe both. I buried my face in her bed sheets and inhaled. Then I reached under her pillow and found her journal.

What did I want to believe? Whether or not I opened the book hinged on the question. Oddly, the possibility that George molested her was not as horrifying as the possibility that she had slept with another boy. If I had been honest, I would have admitted I preferred her suffering to my own.

Having come this far I had to open the journal, but I decided to work backward, from the last entry. Her entries were vague and encrypted in case of parental discovery.

Yesterday: *Got it, going to use it tomorrow to see what's really happening. Cedar fell off his bike at the gas station like a complete retard. I wish I hadn't told him anything.*

The day earlier: *Oh my God, if I didn't have Cedar I don't know what I'd do. I NEED him right now, but what to tell? I'm afraid to tell him everything because maybe he'll fall out of love with me. I couldn't stand the thought of that.*

Come on Kat, get a grip! You just need an expert opinion on this! First, get the thing. Then, if the thing says it's all true, you'll have to go to the place, and then if that's true, then what? Make it disappear? Will I go to Hell? Please, God, give me a sign of what to do!

George's van pulled into the driveway. Having no reasonable escape route, I slid the journal back under the pillow and jumped into Kat's closet. Crouched in a corner I covered myself with stuffed animals and clothes. I could see a sliver of the room through the space between the door and the door frame. I could hear blunted conversation downstairs. Kat made exasperated statements to her mother as she climbed the stairs and entered her room.

Veronica appeared in the doorway. "Take some more boxes, Kat. I really don't think it'll take much effort to get this room packed up today."

"I *told you* I'll get it all packed, *okay?* Don't you have your own crap to worry about? I can get my own boxes. Now leave me alone!" Kat proceeded to throw some random toys and pictures into a box. I wanted to get her attention, but knew she'd scream. The longer I didn't reveal myself, the more my visit turned to voyeurism. I opened my mouth to whisper her name, then shut it. I only hoped she wouldn't start packing the contents of her closet.

George poked his head into the room, loudly singing the Miss America pageant theme, and tossed Kat a roll of packing tape. "For your boxes. Just think, you're going to have your own bathroom. You can dry your undergarments in private or whatever it is you do in there."

"Gross!"

"I'm kidding! Jeez Louise!" George said, then sat down on the edge of the bed. "You wanna talk?"

"About what?"

"It's weird for you. I get that. You and your mom had your life, just the two of you, and I can respect that. It's got to be strange to just one day pick up and move all your stuff. But I want you to feel at home at my place, I really do."

George hesitated then touched Kat's shoulder. She shrugged him off. "Don't touch me. Pervert."

"Why are you calling me that? All right, that's fine. I hope . . . I mean, I just think we had a really good time on the boat, don't you? I want those good times to continue. At *our* house. As a family."

"Leave. Me. Alone."

George sighed, stood, and paused for a second like he was hoping to say something useful, then gave up and left, closing the door gently behind him. Kat listened to him recede down the hall, then reached down between the cushions of her bed, extracted the wand of her pregnancy test, and squinted at it for a while before returning it to its hiding place. "*Fuck,*" she murmured, then threw more things into boxes. Any moment she could open the closet and find me huddled there, but her mother called for her help and she left the room. An hour or so later I heard the van leave the driveway and figured they had all left. I waited a few more minutes then crawled from the closet, listening for signs of life in the house. When I was sure everyone was gone I pulled the pregnancy test from under Kat's mattress to confirm what I already knew. Two stripes, Pregnant.

"What did you do to your lip?" my mom said. "It's bleeding." She handed me a napkin across the table. I dabbed my mouth. The paper flowered with blood.

"Are you chewing your lip?"

"I guess so," I said.

"Must be a habit you picked up when you quit smoking," my dad said to his au gratin potatoes.

"I never smoked."

My parents nodded and sipped their wine. Several times a day my lower lip bled and I applied Blistex, which seemed only to enhance the pain. I tried willing Kat's period into existence. Every morning I called and asked, "Did it happen?" but apart from some misleading discharge, nothing. I read that 30 to 40 precent of pregnancies ended in natural miscarriage within the first trimester. I hoped for a sudden absence of progesterone or some other mysterious biological event to drive the embryo from her womb. I willed the endometrium of her uterus to become necrotic and prostaglandins to kick her uterine smooth muscles into high gear. I could hardly masturbate anymore and when I did it was to the most tawdry and low-grade materials, a JCPenney's underwear catalog, a novelty ballpoint pen that you turned upside down to make the woman's bikini disappear. Kat asked if I could get her a fifth of vodka then punch her several times in the stomach. I told her I wouldn't. After a week of hounding her and still no period she made an appointment at Family Beginnings on the condition that I accompany her.

We rode our bikes together to the clinic, Kat swerving to hit every pothole and bump in the road. I promised that afterward I'd take her to breakfast at Denny's and she could order anything she wanted.

"Are you going to tell them George did it?" I asked.

"Why would I do that? They'd have to report that to the police."

"What are you going to tell them, then? That I did it?"

"I'll make something up."

The Family Beginnings offices were part of a medical complex near a doomed mall that kept shuttering stores. Letters had been stolen from some of the store names on the sign welcoming shoppers into the empty parking lot. A craft store, All That Glitters, was now All That i_ _ _ _s. Apparently the employees had even started answering the phone that way. We parked our bikes behind the clinic by the Dumpsters. The waiting room was mostly empty except for a pregnant Hispanic girl we didn't know. Kat checked in, providing a fake name, and I pawed through a *Newsweek*. The receptionist explained that the first part of the appointment would be a counseling session with someone named April, and then Kat would get an exam.

A voice from the counseling room behind us called out, "Geraldine Ferraro? Is Ms. Ferarro here?"

"That's me," Kat said, and we turned to find our homeroom teacher Mrs. Wheeler standing in front of us with a clipboard in hand.

I wanted to run. Or die. Or escape to our Grand Slam breakfasts. Mrs. Wheeler's face betrayed an instant of recognition quickly replaced by a mild and professional smile. She'd once sent me to the principal's office for showing everybody my sperm, but here, in this clinical context, she'd counter any transgression with a pamphlet. "Come on back," she said.

We followed her to a drab room decorated with a Monet poster that said "MONET" and sat down in front of the desk.

"You weren't expecting to see me," Mrs. Wheeler said. "I volunteer here during the summer. And I want you to know that I don't think anything bad about you for coming here today. In fact, I think you've made a mature decision. What we discuss here is completely confidential. I won't reveal that we had this conversation to anyone, even your parents. I'm here to help. What can I do?"

Kat slowly lifted her eyes. "I think I got pregnant."

"When was your last missed period?"

"Three weeks ago."

"And you had intercourse prior to that time?"

"I . . . it was in Canada. I mean, it wasn't with Cedar. I was on a boat trip with my mom and her boyfriend and there was this town we stopped at. That night my mom and George, the boyfriend, went and got a hotel. To celebrate that they'd gotten engaged. I was supposed to sleep on the boat. I went into the town that night and found these kids at a park and started hanging out with them. They were drinking peach schnapps and asked if I wanted any. I had maybe like a drink and a half of it. So then, one of the boys . . ." Kat paused, her hands shaking. "He was older. I was making out with him and he was like, let's go somewhere together. So I told him about the boat. And we went there. I shouldn't have drunk that schnapps."

Mrs. Wheeler offered a box of tissues while I sat dumbly.

"Have you taken a home pregnancy test?"

"Yes. It was positive."

Mrs. Wheeler asked a few more yes/no questions about sexual activity and drug use and whether Kat understood her options in the event of an unwanted pregnancy.

"I want an abortion," Kat stated. I was surprised at how resolute she sounded.

"Should your test today come up positive, we can refer you to a clinic that performs abortions," Mrs. Wheeler said. "Your next question is probably how much it costs. We have funds to help young women like you. All we ask is that in the future, when you have the means, that you consider making a contribution to Family Beginnings." She let this new pathway sink in a moment then continued, "Do you have any questions, Cedar?" I wondered if she suspected I was really the responsible party here. She knew I was capable of producing sperm, had personally seen them, in fact. I wanted her to know that I was just here to help, but any explanation would have entangled me in Kat's lie. Best to play along. "No," I said.

Kat said quietly, "Mrs. Wheeler? Do you think I'll go to hell if I get the abortion?"

"That's really not something Family Beginnings can address. If you have spiritual questions about abortion, you need to consult with the appropriate person at your church. But Katie, I will tell you it's ultimately your decision alone to make."

Mrs. Wheeler's answer seemed inadequate to me, something she had rehearsed from a manual. Kat asked if I could be in the room during her exam and Mrs. Wheeler showed us to the examination room. She said a nurse would be in shortly and that Kat needed to put on a robe. Then Mrs. Wheeler's decorum fell away and she took us each under one of her arms and said, "It's going to be okay." Then she took a moment to compose herself, smiled tightly, and left the room.

I watched Kat undress and found it odd how nonsexual she looked in her nakedness. She was in a body, undergoing processes, needing diagnosis. The nurse was a wide, red-faced woman who conducted this business without much enthusiasm. Kat climbed onto the table and the nurse drew some blood. Then she spread her legs as directed, sucking air through her teeth when the nurse inserted the speculum. The nurse explained that every pregnancy test they administered was accompanied by tests for a variety of STDs—gonorrhea, chlamydia, herpes, etcetera. She inserted a long wooden swab into the opening of the speculum. When it was done the nurse flatly wished us the best of luck and left. Kat wiped the gel from her vagina and tossed the paper towel into the trash. I felt extraneous to this solemn and antiseptic ceremony. What could I, of all people, possibly do to help her now?

I helped Kat in through the front door of the clinic and toward the nearest chair. Her feet benumbed by Valium, her sneakers dragged across the carpet. The instructions had been to take two the night before and one that morning, but she'd done the opposite. On the bus she had washed the two pills down with Sprite and her body had turned limp and slumped against mine.

The clinic was empty except for a couple of receptionists. I recognized the music in the background as Steely

Dan, a band I had always hated. The rubber fetus–bearing protestors I'd feared hadn't materialized, but the cheeriness of the lobby suggested peace on the verge of disruption. After helping Kat sign in, we sat beneath the boughs of a plastic plant. Within minutes a female nurse called her back.

The duration of an abortion is about the length of time it takes to read one issue of *Newsweek* from cover to cover. I wanted to run across the street to the gas station and buy cigarettes, but feared Kat would emerge from the swinging doors as soon as I left. So I stayed and learned about Berlin's reunification and the new James Bond movie. In my mind, beneath the blathering text of newsworthy items, chanted a chorus: *my girlfriend is getting an abortion, my girlfriend is getting, my girlfriend, an abortion, my girlfriend is getting.* Steely Dan was followed by Hall and Oates singing "One on One," the Cars doing "Drive," and a-ha's "Take On Me." My surroundings seemed to lack the basic requirements of reality. A director could have called "Cut!" and I wouldn't have been all that surprised.

An elderly couple arrived and spent a lot of time going over their paperwork, the man breathing with assistance from his portable oxygen tank. I was pretty sure they weren't here for the same kind of procedure we were here for. What would they think if they learned what was occurring this moment behind the swinging door? When Kat finally appeared in front of me she was smiling, startling me. The nurse spoke to me about how much rest Kat needed, how many pills to take, when to eat. I nodded as if everything made sense while my drugged girlfriend wobbled beside me.

"They gave me something pretty potent!" Kat said when we were outside. I wanted to ask her how it went, but the question felt more appropriate for somebody who'd just completed a job interview. She said, "It wasn't as bad as I thought. The doctor was really nice. At the end he said, 'Well, you used to be pregnant, and now you aren't.' He said to eat soup."

"I'll get you some when we get to your house," I said, as we walked our bikes through an alley to the bus stop. I checked the schedule and saw we'd have to wait half an hour.

Kat sat down on the bench, rummaged in her big knit bag and pulled out her Walkman, inserting Def Leppard's *Hysteria*. "Don't be mad at me because I just want to listen to music."

"I won't. Go ahead."

The bus came and I strapped the bikes to the front rack. The bus squeezed us slowly through one development after another until we came to Kat's old neighborhood. There was a FOR RENT sign in the yard with a picture of a big-haired woman's head on it. Kat used her extra key to get in. The empty house echoed around us as we climbed the stairs to her old bedroom, where that morning I had stashed a couple sleeping bags and pillows. She lay down and I waited until she was snoring, then went to the grocery store four blocks away. I selected a couple cans of chicken noodle soup and a six pack of 7UP. Day-to-day banality continued unabated for the rest of the world. No one, not the butcher, the clerks, or the old lady frowning over the bananas knew that my girlfriend had gotten an abortion that morning. Stupidly, I almost expected the entire world to pause and reflect on this occasion. But the same benign rituals of buying proceeded uninterrupted and, thrust into them, I found myself confounded and alone.

When I returned to Kat's old house I realized that I had no way of preparing the soup or even opening the cans. I hunted through the empty cupboards hoping to find a left-behind can opener, but everything was gone. I sheepishly went upstairs to tell Kat I'd screwed up. She was still asleep, drooling onto a He-Man Masters of the Universe pillow case. We were finally alone together in a place ideal for having sex. I internally scolded myself for the thought. I imagined George's middle-aged body slurping against hers. Where was Veronica when it happened? An imaginary detective led me through the cabin of George's boat. They started here, see, and he laid her down on this mattress here. The reality of it screwed up my stomach. I tasted blood on my lips.

While Kat slept I curled beside her and stared at a corner where a wisp of cobweb swayed in a draft. I boiled at what George had done to my girlfriend, but the anger possessed another dimension I was slow to admit. Disgusted with myself, with Kat, and with George, my thoughts endlessly looping visions of intercourse and anatomical dissections, I came to admit that what coursed through me was jealousy. He had so easily accomplished things with Kat that I had long wanted to do. I was jealous of a rapist. I wanted to kill myself.

The afternoon gave in to a lackluster dusk. I knew my parents must have been wondering where I was, but part of me wanted to get busted so the whole story could come tumbling out. I indulged my imagination with my suicide, my limp body in the tub, their wailed regrets. I felt Kat looking at me and turned my head.

"I'm hungry. Did you get the soup?" she asked.

"Yeah, but there's no can opener."

"What else did you get?"

"7UP."

"That's it?"

"Yeah."

"Thanks a lot, Cedar. Thanks a lot."

"I didn't know there was no can opener."

"What have you been doing this whole time? You could've at least gone out and gotten something else."

"I was watching you. Fine. I'll go get more food."

Misconception

I left abruptly, slamming the front door behind me. I help my girlfriend abort a child molester's baby and she gets all bitchy. Fuck it. The closest fast food was a Wendy's on the other side of the elementary school. I left my bike at Kat's and crossed through the ball fields where a day camp was engaged in a series of elaborate relay races. There were kids in matching baggy T-shirts, orange traffic cones demarcating some kind of course, and frisbees and whistles.

I ordered a couple Frostys, a chicken sandwich, a double bacon cheeseburger, a bowl of chili, two orders of fries, and a salad. As I waited for my order I watched a mopey, acne-defeated girl stuffed into her uniform clean the salad bar with a rag. Two cooler-looking girls in Esprit shirts walked by, one of them digging her hand into the crouton bin. The employee quickly grabbed the girl's wrist, and said, "Hey, you can't do that." The crouton thief jerked away, laughing, popping croutons into her mouth. "I didn't mean it," the employee said sadly. I tried to imagine her life. She probably had a mundane daily routine, a mother who watched soaps, a father who worked at a plant or factory. She wanted friends, I could tell; she was just confused about the whole system of friendship. She never said the right things around other girls and was always a step or two behind in fashion and music. She earned straight *B*s, was the last to get picked for teams, suffered the indignity of her mother taking her shopping for cosmetics at the drug store. She ate chocolate in her room at night reading

Sweet Valley High books. She would go to a community college, become a secretary at an office, marry a man similarly stymied by social rituals. They'd watch TV and make love—concurrently, not sequentially. They'd have a kid, an average student, undistinguished on the playfield or classroom, a kid who would represent the boring and unimaginative section of the gene pool. I could feel contempt for such a person, for such a *nobody*, but this high school girl whose name tag read "Beth" had rendered me incapable of anything but unbearable, knife-twisting empathy when she said, "I didn't mean it." She would have suspended her salad bar duties and her adherence to the rules of Wendy's if it had meant someone being nice to her, and this made me terribly sad. I wanted to say something kind to her, but she returned to the inner sanctum of the kitchen and my order came up.

As I was walking across the parking lot with my bag of food and the drink carrier, my parents pulled up in their Volvo. Without thinking, I got in. We were all surprised to see each other. The interior of the car reeked of an argument. My mom was in the driver's seat, meaning my dad had gone on strike from driving because he would no longer tolerate my mother's commentary on his substandard traffic-safety skills. We sat silent in the parking lot for a good minute. A woman wearing bright floral stretch pants entered the Wendy's, slapping one of her kids on the head on the way in.

"We've driven all over this goddamn town looking for you," my dad said.

"Are you going to tell us where you were all day?" my mother said.

"Hanging out," I said.

"You missed Mr. Dickman's lawn. He called and asked why you didn't show," my mom said.

"I was just getting something to eat."

My mom's eyes tightened in the rear view mirror. "Why two beverages?"

"I was taking one to Kat."

"She lives nearby, doesn't she? Let's drive there." My mom put the car in gear and sped out of the parking lot. The sharpness with which she cut corners, the emphatic way she hit the brakes, all of it was a mechanical extension of a fight that had commenced between my parents, and we had to endure it with our stomachs climbing up out of our rib cages.

"We know you're sneaking out to fool around with Kat," my dad said.

"Stop the car, I'm going to throw up," I said.

My mother pulled over. She turned around in her seat and yelled at me. "What the hell are you hiding?"

I became unmistakably a boy. My mouth twisted into an awful grimace as I started to sob. Whatever argument my parents had been enduring deteriorated into their personal record books of fights won and lost as they attended to my sorrows. And what a shit I was for even crying about it at all; it wasn't as though I was the one who'd just gotten the abortion. I told them everything between heaving sobs —the boat trip, the clinics, the empty house. For the first time in months they quietly listened to me. My dad even reached back and touched my head, then slid his palm down to my cheek and wiped a tear with his thumb. They said they believed me that the pregnancy hadn't been my doing, and agreed to drive me to Kat's old place. My mother said she would take care of everything and not tell Kat's parents. My dad promised to buy a can opener. When we arrived at the house Kat was gone.

When I called Tuesday night Kat's mom answered, picking up the phone while laughing at something. Still chuckling she said hello. I almost hung up but feared Veronica would have been able to recognize me by the sound of my breathing. I asked for Kat.

"I'm sorry, Katie's asleep. She said she wasn't feeling well. But say, when are you going to come by and see the new place? We should have you over for dinner again. George? What do you think about inviting Cedar over for dinner one of these nights?"

I agreed to come over that Friday and hung up the cheap phone I'd won in a fund-raising drive. My parents mumbled in the kitchen, a low boil of conversation. I decided I wouldn't leave my room tonight, and would distract myself with physiology texts. I opened a volume, bored and distracted barely a paragraph into it. My mom knocked on my door and said through the wood, "Cedar, we need to talk to you."

"I really would like to be left alone right now, thanks."

"This can't wait. Meet us in the kitchen."

I extracted myself from my bed and stood in the center of my room remembering a story I'd heard once about some kid's older brother who was on antipsychotic medication. One night he had taken a couple of his pills and spent three hours crawling from one side of his living room to the other to retrieve a bottle cap. When I'd heard the story I had been appalled by the idea, but now that degree of sedation sounded like a pretty swell time.

I found my parents seated at opposite sides of the dinette table, looking serious. I was sure they were going to launch into me about how I had handled this whole abortion event, ground me, make me see a shrink, whatever.

"Your mother and I are separating."

The sentence landed. We were all silent for a good period of time. Then my dad continued with the logistics, saying he was moving to a house in the city, that I would stay here with my mom, that my wishes about visitation and living arrangements would be welcomed, something about lawyers, something about child-care payments.

Something about none of this being my fault. They expected me to cry so I tried not to. Maybe if time had been rewound and Kat had never gotten pregnant and had an abortion, maybe then I would have been able to coolly assess the situation, but that they had chosen this day of all days to make their little announcement cracked what rickety scaffolding I was using to hold myself together and I cried for the second time, like a little kid again, hating myself for indulging their expectation that I would cry, an expectation reinforced by the incongruous box of facial tissue standing at the ready next to the salt and pepper shakers.

"Fuck you!" I said. "Fuck both of you."

I locked myself in my room and barred the door with my dresser, though they could have gotten in had they really wanted to. When I was about ten I used to play a trick on my parents, crawling between my mattress and the box spring of my bed. At first my mom had scolded me, saying I could suffocate, but the mattress wasn't really that heavy. I had "tricked" them this way every night for a few months when they tucked me in. My dad would come into the room and say, "Gee, where's Cedar? I thought he was in here," and as I giggled he would sigh and sit lightly on the bed, saying, "I guess I'll just rest here on Cedar's bed until he comes back. Boy, am I ever sleepy." As he increased his weight on the mattress, I would giggle more until he leaped up and pulled the mattress away and exclaim that he'd found me. Tonight I crawled under the mattress for the first time in years and choked in darkness.

The next day Paul met me at the train trestle over the river. I immediately demanded a cigarette. Absurdly, he had grown a mustache since I'd last seen him, if you could call the wispy insect legs sprouting at various angles from his upper lip a mustache.

"What the hell is that on your lip?"

"Oh, this?" Paul said, stroking the 'stache. "It's my pussy tickler, bro."

It felt good to laugh, but I didn't laugh long. Leaning against the rail I gazed into the hypnotic brown eddies below. I told him about my parents, holding off on the Kat stuff to see how he'd respond. "Do you think your mom and dad would let me stay at your place for awhile? While my folks iron things out?"

Paul put his arm around my shoulder and gave it a pat. The gesture seemed like a kid mimicking an adult, or mimicking something seen on TV. I shrugged him off. "Kat stopped talking to me."

"Yeah, man, I'm sorry. I heard what happened."

"Who told you?"

"Her name starts with *M* and rhymes with Men At Work's hit album *Cargo*."

"What did she say?"

"She said Kat and you broke up."

I squeezed the rusty railing and watched the blood disappear from my hands. "I'm just going to kill myself now."

"What happened? I thought you guys were doing great."

"She never told me we broke up."

"Ooops."

My empty stomach squeezed its bile. I had only eaten an English muffin that day. More blood on my lips. I told Paul I'd be at his house around dinner time then got on my bike and pedaled across town to Kat's new house. I knew the neighborhood, and found the place by recognizing Veronica's car. As I walked up to the door, Veronica came around the side of the house with a gardening bucket full of weeds.

"Cedar! You made it over here. Let's go in, I want to show you the new place."

I followed Kat's mom into the split-level, staring dumbly at the panty line through her stretch pants as we ascended to the living room. There was already an Olan Mills portrait of Veronica, George, and Kat hanging above the mantle. They were all smiling like idiots in front of a fake forest background, wearing matching green sweaters. Unbelievable. George's hand was on Kat's shoulder. Fucking child molester.

"Katie! Your friend Cedar's here! I'll fix us some lemonade, yeah?"

"That sounds great," I said.

Kat emerged from her bedroom down the hall and looked at me incredulously.

"How come you won't talk to me?" I whispered.

"I can't believe you just showed up like this."

I followed Kat to her bedroom. "Can't I visit my girlfriend? Or did I miss the fact that we're not going out anymore?"

"You should have gotten the message."

"You should have told me to my face you wanted to break up." I looked around Kat's new room, easily twice the size of her old one. "You like living here with your new pervert dad?"

"You should just leave."

"I'm not leaving until you explain why you want to break up. After all that shit I went through for the abortion."

"Quit talking so loud."

I repeated, whispering, "After all the shit I went through for the abortion."

"All the shit *you* went through? That was *my* thing. It's not *your* thing. I get to live in my body. You get to have your rich parents pay your way through college, and become a lawyer or some shit. You get to forget about everything."

"But I *won't* forget. Kat, please, don't break up with me. Not right now, okay? My parents are getting divorced."

"Lemonade!" Veronica called.

118

"I can't take care of your problems right now," Kat said. "In a second, Mom!"

"You don't even care. My dad's moving out this week. They don't even give a shit where I end up."

Kat squinted and gave me the kind of disgusted look pioneered by fourteen-year-old girls. "Now you know what it's like for the rest of us, Cedar."

To be polite, I drank lemonade and ate shortbread cookies with Kat and her mother on the weathered deck overlooking an overgrown backyard. Somehow I managed to have a conversation with Veronica about her landscaping plans. Mowing lawns had made me some kind of expert. I heard myself expressing opinions on fertilizer. A tangle of verbs and nouns strained against the roof of my mouth, *How's it feel to know your fiancé raped your daughter? Oh, Kat didn't tell you?* but I only talked of bulbs and weed killer.

"Well, are you going to tell him?" Veronica asked Kat.

"Tell him what?"

"You know. About Labor Day?"

"My mom and George are going to have a wedding."

"That's great," I said.

"Nothing fancy, just a service at St. Matthew's and a reception at the All-Purpose Hall," Veronica said. "Katie is going to be my maid of honor. You should come, Cedar!"

"I wouldn't want to miss it," I said.

Veronica picked up our plates and glasses and, humming, returned them to the kitchen. Kat and I listened to birds, not saying anything. I wanted to tell her I was sorry about everything, but her dumping me erected a stubborn barrier against my sympathies.

"Are you happy now?" Kat said.

"About what?"

"About getting invited to the wedding?"

"Yeah, where's the honeymoon? In your bedroom?"

"Fuck you. You think you know everything about my life but you know shit. You have no idea who I even am."

"I think I'm going to kill myself. Yeah, do you all a favor."

"Shut up, Cedar. You're not going to kill yourself."

"At least I didn't kill a baby."

What happened next was so sudden it took my mind several attempts to assemble the sequence. I looked down and saw the front of my shirt covered with blood. Kat stood over me, breathing hard. Slowly, my nose started to throb. Then I understood that's where the blood was coming from. I choked, spit up some blood that had gone down the back of my throat. Kat's fist was still clenched. She had decked me pretty hard.

"I'm going home now," I said.

Our house was a fissure, a widening wound. It was the middle of the day so I knew my parents would be at work.

My dad had been sleeping on a futon in the guest bed-room, where several boxes had begun to accrete his be-longings. His extraction from the house had been slowed by the daily bullshit routines to which he had to hew, and his effects looked haphazardly gathered. A half-eaten candy bar sat sheathed in its frayed wrapper on the desk. I imag-ined my dad setting it there, chewing as he slipped books and old Christmas presents into these dull brown cubes. The candy bar looked grotesque to me, the byproduct of some foul and biological process. There was nothing in this room I needed. I went to my bedroom and threw clothes and an anatomy text in a duffel. I needed some bathroom things. My toothbrush looked like it had been dragged behind a car, its bristles flattened and falling out. I imag-ined it sitting beside the Dillses' toothbrushes and Paul making fun of me about it. We kept a stock of new tooth-brushes in the bathroom downstairs, which had been trans-formed into my mom's darkroom, with an enlarger sitting on the toilet and dried pictures hanging from a cord stretched between the shower curtain rod and a hook on the opposite wall. I rummaged through the drawers for the dental supplies. A line of photographs hung behind me, reflected backward in the mirror. I expected to see the usual hair and mucus textures of my mom's work, but these looked like candid shots of people.

They were pictures of my dad meeting his girlfriend outside a restaurant. In one he stood with his head turned expectantly, looking down the block. A woman approaching; an embrace. There is a kiss. Next, he's got his hand on her ass and they're entering the restaurant. Then they're coming back out, smiling. A couple shots of them talking. Another kiss, my dad's hands cradling her face. Then a zoom on her, a close-up as she clears strands of hair from her eyes. She's much younger than my dad, with dark straight hair and big eyes, breasts distorting the ridges of her sweater. Another shot of her walking away, her back, her skirt stretched over the two promontories of her ass.

I removed this last picture from the line, set it on the sink, and beat off onto it.

When I finished washing up I crumpled the comed-on photo into a ball and stuffed it into the kitchen garbage under a pile of honeydew rinds. I left a note to my parents addressed "To Whom It May Concern," informing them I'd be staying at Paul's.

Paul's house was a riot of kids, dogs, and the massive medieval-role-playing props his parents used at weekend Renaissance fairs. At one point some officials from the city had ordered them to dismantle the backyard trebuchet after neighbor complaints. Not that their neighbors had much room to complain. The Dills lived in a real-estate agent's nightmare of a yellow house with railroad tracks on one side and a halfway house for ex-cons on the other.

Across the tracks was a vegetable processing factory that clanked and screeched at all hours. On the other side of the halfway house was a fire station. Paul's house managed to feel like some sort of haven amid this madness.

Paul's mom Henrietta was morbidly obese, north of three hundred pounds. She sweated in her thin housedress on the couch playing lute or making the kids castles from yogurt containers and pipe cleaners. They had no TV, by choice. Occasionally, one of Paul's younger brothers would get hurt and run crying to be comforted in the folds of Henrietta's girth. Various dogs and cats from other neighborhoods prowled the living room. Every time I visited, Paul's dad Sven was busy with some gigantic project, ripping insulation out of the attic or troubleshooting the septic tank, his red afro atop an expression of intense concentration, eyes obscured behind the thick lenses of his glasses. When I walked up the driveway past chalked hopscotch schema and abandoned toy cars he pulled off his gloves and came over to pat me on the back.

"I understand your folks are going through some rough times," Sven said. "You're welcome here as long as you need to stay. And as long as it's okay with your mom and dad."

"Thanks, Sven," I said, then entered the house. Paul's two little brothers were whacking each other with foam swords, in the nude.

"Cedar! Hugs!" Henrietta exclaimed. I came up behind her on the couch and wrapped my arms around her shoulders.

Everything about her physical appearance should have revolted me—her hairy armpits and shoulders studded with
skin tags—but I recognized only the same warmth of welcome I had always felt at this house. Paul came downstairs
in his Stormtrooper mask, gave me the double middle-
finger salute, farted theatrically, and launched himself onto
an easy chair. Paul's brother Douglas whapped his brother
Bertrand a little too hard on the side of the head. Bertrand
stood in the middle of the living room, his face frozen in a
silent prescream, then released his wail.

While Henrietta attended to the little boys, I followed
Paul upstairs to the unfinished addition to their house, his
room. The walls were still Sheetrock, the floors exposed
plywood. The Dills had gone a little crazy with the sky-
lights, studding the ceiling with bubblelike protrusions of
molded plastic. Whether the family ever intended to complete this part of their house was anyone's guess, but Paul
seemed to like it this way. Later, when I thought of my
childhood, I would envision it unfolding in this room, with
bags of Cheetos and off-brand colas, Paul and I poring
over the handouts Henrietta used in the classes where she
taught sex ed to retarded people.

"Check out what my parents bought me," Paul said,
tossing a *High Society* magazine my way.

"You're kidding."

"No, man. My mom asked if I was interested in pornography. We had a big discussion about it. They think that if

124

they give it to me now it won't become a big deal later on. Some kind of parenting-book crap like that. Whatever. Just check out the aureole on the chick on page eighty-nine. I've been using it to try to come."

"Any luck with that?"

"Almost," Paul said. "I think."

I leafed through the magazine, unaroused at the air-brushed and stapled flesh. I set it down.

"What happened to your nose?" Paul said.

"Kat punched me."

"Wow, I guess you guys really are broken up."

"I told her she killed a baby," I said, then remembered I hadn't let Paul in on any of the abortion stuff. Now I had to tell him. Shocked and fascinated, he listened to the story. At one point Douglas crawled up the steps to spy on us, eliciting a wave of action-figure-throwing retribution from Paul, more crying and yelling from downstairs, and a reprimand from Henrietta. Scent tendrils of spaghetti sauce crawled up from the kitchen. I told Paul I wanted George dead. The phone rang. Sven said it was my mother.

"We got your note," my mom said.

"That's nice."

"How long were you intending to stay at Paul's?"

"I don't know."

"Well, thank Paul's mom for me, okay?" she said. I hung up disappointed she hadn't begged me to come home.

Misconception

During dinner I pretended to laugh at the Dills's family jokes, their gross stories and observations about human flatulence. At one point Sven detailed his vasectomy. I wondered if my parents were sitting down for dinner together and imagined complete silence between them. When we finished I volunteered to do the dishes. Paul was ordered to join me in the disaster of a kitchen, where dusty bunches of dried peppers and garlic hung from the ceiling and an exotic bottle of Asian liquor on the windowsill pickled a dead lizard.

"Get this," I said. "Veronica invited me to her and George's wedding."

"Unbelievable," Paul said.

"I'm thinking of going. You know, show up, pig out on free food, embarrass Kat in front of everybody."

"If you're going to kill George, that would be the perfect time to do it," Paul said.

"Who said anything about killing George?"

"You did. You said you wanted to kill him."

"Shut up. You know what I meant by saying I want to kill somebody. You say you want to kill your brothers all the time. Not *kill* kill."

"Yeah, but what if you did kill him? How would you do it?"

I thought a while. "Poison?"

"At the wedding? Like poison the punch or something? Nah, you wouldn't want to risk killing anyone else. Just the sicko child molester. God, it just hit me that that's really what he is. He really did that to Kat? Unbelievable."

"Maybe we could get a gun."

"What, you're just going to walk up to him at his wedding and blow him away? Don't you want to do it and not get caught?"

"It's not like I'd go to regular jail. Just juvie. You can still take high school classes there."

"You're not going to shoot George."

"I know I'm not. But what if."

"Where's the wedding taking place?"

"Some church. Then a reception at All-Purpose Hall. Kat's going to be the maid of honor. Thing is, if I made him admit at the wedding that he did what he did to Kat, nobody would care if I shot him. They'd probably give me a standing ovation."

"Yeah, make him get on his knees and admit he's a rapist."

"Then shoot him right there. Everybody would want me to do it anyway. The witnesses would all say it was self-defense or whatever. They'd know I killed him because he had it coming."

"Revenge," Paul said.

"Better than revenge," I said, "retribution."

"You're not going to kill him," Paul said.

"Yeah," I said, "but I know somebody who would."

Across mountains.

The next foggy morning while the Dills slept I gathered my belongings in a backpack and rode to the ferry terminal, locking my bike next to the sleek rides of the commuters. I boarded the ferry and sat in a corner of the sun deck with adults reading newspapers and drinking tea from travel mugs. Slowly Seattle came into view, building by building as if from a dreaming mind. I joined the flow of people leaving the boat, hoping to avoid anyone I knew. Then it was up the hill to the Greyhound station, past men sleeping in the doorways of buildings, fresh-haired professional women on their way to work, department store displays full of fur coats and camping equipment. At the station I bought a ticket across the mountains. I wore my baseball hat down low hoping it would make me look older, and it seemed to work. The guy behind the counter didn't appear to think twice about issuing me a ticket. The bus would leave in an hour, so I waited in the Burger King next door. I imagined Paul waking up, realizing I had left, discovering my thank-you note on the kitchen table. I had written that I was heading home, and thanked them for all the awesome food. Right about now my parents were emerging from their separate rooms, mouthing some meaningless niceties at each other over coffee, then parsing through their collective belongings. I'd call them later that day and pretend I was calling from the mall. Assuming I was still staying at Paul's, they wouldn't suspect I was actually calling from a rest stop. I was doing them a favor, getting out of their way while they dealt with the marital jetsam that needed to be codified into documents, agreements, and mutual understandings. My absence was convenient to them, making it easier to justify the mistake they were about to make. My whereabouts would be the least of their worries.

Boarding call. As the bus pulled away I pressed my forehead against the window. The diesel muscle of the engine was an affirmation that I had actually decided to find Kat's father. The freeway made it more real, and then the hills, penetrated by speeding vehicles. We breached the pass and in thinning foliage and the gentle gradation of earth tones from green to brown, Washington state exposed its dual nature. As I stared through my smudged reflection at the landscape, I had no idea how I was going to find Kat's father, or where I would stay that night. The Greyhound deposited me at the station. I found a phone book hanging from a cable in a booth and scanned the Daniels. Alden Daniels. Carol Daniels. Pete Daniels. SW Daniels. No Jerry Daniels. I called Alden. Disconnected or no longer in service. Carol Daniels's answering machine said she was away from the phone teaching piano lessons and to leave a message after the F sharp. A girl at Pete Daniels's place answered and said she knew no one named Jerry. SW Daniels didn't pick up.

I turned to the yellow-pages listings for septic system repair services. A woman's voice at Apex Septic said, "Apex Septic, the pumper for your dumper. How can I assist you today?" She confirmed that a Jerry Daniels worked there, but it was his day off. I asked for his number but she said giving out employee numbers was against policy since an incident involving a mechanic's child-support payments. I begged for the number, said I was a friend who had come all the way across the Cascades to see him.

"Tell you what. You give me the number you're at, and I'll call him and tell him to give you a call."

"Tell him it's important. It's about his daughter, Kat."

I gave the woman the phone booth's number and settled onto a bench. Hissing buses arrived and departed. I bought some items from a nearby vending machine. An hour passed. I read a newspaper that looked like it had been mauled. Another hour. For some reason it never occurred to me to call Apex Septic again. Instead, I waited. I had proved this trip was futile. I had come unprepared. And why hadn't I just tried calling Kat's dad to begin with instead of coming all the way over here in person? I forgot to call my parents. The phone rang.

"Is this Cedar? Kat's boyfriend?"

"Yeah. I need to talk to you."

"Where you at?"

"Greyhound station."

"I'll be there in ten."

As Jerry walked in, he chucked a soda cup into the nearest waste can, missed the shot, and neglected to pick up the cup. Unlike the time I had first met him, he was in no mood to impress anybody. He wore his face as a form of protection, not for expression, avoiding eye contact unless absolutely necessary. He'd dressed in the kind of torn jeans, flannel, and Stihl chainsaw hat that years later rock stars would wear. I followed him to his pickup and he suggested a nearby restaurant he called a greasy spoon. He ordered coffee and I ordered coffee, too. Then he slapped his hand on the table and said, "What's this about? I know it ain't good."

"I came all the way over here to tell you this, because as Kat's dad I thought you should know."

"Spit it out, son."

"Veronica is getting married to this guy George, who has been abusing Kat."

"What do you mean by abusing."

"He raped her. She got pregnant. She had to get an abortion."

Nothing changed in Jerry's expression. I almost expected him to say "So what?" After half a minute of silence he said, "Does Veronica know?"

"Kat hasn't told her anything."

"And this George guy. You're sure this is the case?"

"Well, yeah. He and Veronica are getting married on Labor Day."

"Okay. Well. Thanks for telling me all this, I guess."

"I thought you should know."

"I wish I didn't but I'm glad you told me. Fine then. I've got to get myself to church."

Some Mexican farm laborers arrived at the restaurant. Jerry watched them over his shoulder until they had all settled at the counter.

"Think I could take those guys?" Jerry said.

"The ones who just came in?"

"Yeah. Problem is, though, they stick tight with their kin. Fifteen cousins to a family. Mess with one bean and you get the whole burrito."

"Do you know somewhere I could stay the night?" I said.

"You don't have a motel somewhere? You planning on sleeping in the park if you didn't find me?" he paused. "Veronica, that bitch. Man oh man."

"I was thinking I'd see about a youth hostel."

"You can crash at my place. Fuck it. Looks like church is a wash."

On the way to his place, Jerry seemed to speak just to kill the silence. He wanted me to know about his "little theory."

"I don't know if this is even what you'd call an original idea or anything. I was installing a Mopar cam on a Chevy when I thought of it. I think I was holding a socket wrench, and I started thinking about how the wrench itself had to of been made in a factory. And that factory was full of machines that were put together with other tools. Then those tools were made by other machines, in other factories, back in time. And at some point in the past, the machines had to of been made with tools that had been made by human hands. And before that, there had to be other, simpler tools to make the newer, better tools. And how the very first metal tools had to of been made with tools made out of something else, like stone, maybe? At one point there were just human hands making things out of rocks, but those rocks led step-by-step to today's huge factories full of complex machines and, eventually, Mopar cams. You can point to any tool and know that it's part of a family tree that started with bare human hands."

Jerry lived in a little house that he said had once been a shack for migrant workers. It had been renovated half a dozen times, the living room comprising the entirety of the old house. He pointed to a board nailed to the ceiling where a tin chimney used to go. The floor was a jigsaw of stitched-together carpet samples. Wood paneled walls held a dozen or so paint-by-numbers wildlife scenes. Jerry nodded to a brown vinyl couch with stuffing coming out of the arms. "You can take the couch tonight."

"Thanks. You have a nice place."

"Whatever, dude. You're not fooling anybody. But think of it this way—four families used to live in this here living room."

Jerry offered me a can of Oly beer and I tried to act like it wasn't a big deal. He tossed it to me from the kitchen. It slipped from my hands and fell behind the couch. After fishing it out and wiping the lint from it, I cracked the can and slurped the foam running over the edges, over my fingers.

"I know what you're thinking," he said. "I'm off the wagon, and fuck you for noticing. You like movies?"

"Sure."

"Don't tell anyone, but I've got HBO coming in here for free. I tape the movies I like for later. What kind do you like? I got *Mad Max, Terminator, Rambo* . . ."

"*Rambo*'s good."

"Shit yeah. That's a classic."

From a molded-plastic case beside the TV Jerry withdrew a video camera with a shoulder pack. After fiddling with a couple cables, he got the movie to show up. It took me a minute to figure out why it looked funny. Instead of taping the movie directly from the TV, he had set the camera on his coffee table and aimed it at the set while the movie played. The sound was horrible, and five minutes in the tape showed Jerry walking in front of the camera wearing sweatpants.

When the movie concluded, I asked the question I had been holding for the past few hours. "Do you think you'll try to get custody of Kat?"

Jerry breathed in through his teeth. "That's a tough one, Cedar. Fact is, I know she wouldn't be thrilled with the idea. Her mom's been able to provide her a lot more than I ever could. Look at this place. Can you imagine Katie moving in here?"

"But what about George?"

Jerry pulled the lever on his recliner, propelling his body up and to a standing position. "Yeah, okay, let's look at this situation here. You come on over on a Greyhound to drop this bomb on me, and I guess what I'm thinking is, a guy's gonna take his time figuring out the best course of action in a case like this. I can't just get in my truck and swoop down and take her away with me. You should know this. You were there last time I talked to her. She hates my guts, and truth be told she has good reasons to. It's not as easy as you think. There's fuckin' lawyers to deal with. Hearings and shit. Any cocksucker with a dick can become a dad, but when you *stop* being a parent, that's when things get real complicated. I'm getting another beer. You?"

"Okay."

"You're sure Veronica doesn't know?"

"I'm not sure."

"Because if she doesn't know about what happened, then that's the step you gotta take before I get involved. Knowing her, she won't stand for that shit. I don't care if the guy drives a Caddy and has a country-club membership, the moment Veronica finds out, they're outta there. Trust me."

"What if Veronica already knows?"

The volume of Jerry's voice dropped. "Then things are a lot worse than I think."

Halfway through the second beer, I began to feel it. I pressed my head back against the couch and closed my eyes. Then I said, "My parents are getting a divorce."

"That's the pits, no two ways about it."

"My dad's just taking off, moving into the city with his new girlfriend or something."

"Sucks."

"It's like he stopped giving a shit."

Jerry put his hand on my knee. "This is going to sound like bullshit, but you gotta trust me. He does give a shit. I'm sure he's thinking of you all the time. He's probably embarrassed about the whole thing. He's probably scared to face you. He'll get in touch, I promise. And when he does, he's going to expect you to be pissed. How could you not be? But at some point, not right away, you gotta give your old man a second chance. Trust me, you never stop loving a kid."

Maybe it was the beer? The weird house? The long day traveling? Whatever it was, I started to cry. Jerry held me tight to his flannel chest. After a few minutes, I could have stopped myself, but instead I refreshed my grief, pictured my father again, and wrung the remaining tears from my insides.

And then Jerry drank another beer. He slipped in another video, *The Road Warrior*. A few minutes in, he freeze-framed it, smudgy lines jiggling across the image, and pressed his finger against the screen. "See," he said, "if you look close you can see that dude's got a titty picture pasted to his rig."

I wanted to get out of this crappy house and into the warm, carpeted interior of a Greyhound. Jerry sat trapped in the movie's gaze, overreacting to it with whoops, spilling his beer, offering me another. I said no and went to the bathroom to piss. Atop the toilet bowl sat a stack of well-thumbed porno mags with exotic names unlike the ones you could get at a gas station. I held on to the edge of the sink and peed. Jerry banged hard on the bathroom door with his fists and I jumped, the stream arcing over the lip of the toilet, hitting the wall. Jerry laughed on the other side. "Just messing with you, bro. I'm gonna make me up some tacos. You up for that?"

In the living room Mad Max battled punk rockers in the outback for oil. Jerry turned his refrigerator inside out, taco fixings strewn over his already cluttered kitchen counter. He poured vegetable oil into a pan and fired it up, then started making shells. He stopped in the middle of chopping onions and pointed the knife at me. "That fuck hole. He's gonna burn for what he did to my little girl." He whacked at the pile of irregularly cut-up onions some more, then spun around, onion tears welling in his eyes. "You tell me. You ever fuck my little girl?"

"No. No."

Jerry grabbed me by the front of my shirt and lifted me off the ground, setting me down facing the stove. I groaned. My reflection wobbled in the heating oil. He stabbed the knife into the cutting board and pushed my head down toward the pan. "Did you fuck her? You know you fucked her, you little shit. Did you fuck her?"

I struggled out of Jerry's grip and fell against the kitchen table, scattering piles of newspapers, tools, crap. He picked up the knife again and laughed as he continued chopping. "Ah, I know you haven't, man. I was just fucking with you."

"That wasn't funny."

"You like whole beans or refried?"

"I should go."

"Aw, come on."

"You're drunk."

"I'm not! Fucking! Drunk!" Jerry's voice pounded the walls. I ran through the living room, grabbed my backpack, and flew out the door, across the lawn to the street. Behind me Jerry yelled from the doorway, "Come on, man. Hey! I'm sorry. I'm sorry!"

The houses in this neighborhood were spread out and I had no clue which way to go, so I ran in the direction of the greatest emanation of light. Slowly, the houses began crowding closer together and a Chevron station appeared, its sign a beacon. Panting, I fell into the phone booth and spent a good ten minutes crying. When I recovered I said, "Okay, okay, okay," and tried to formulate a plan. I needed to get into the city. I needed a cab. I called the first cab company in the phone book and told them the names of the nearest street signs. While I waited I bought a prepackaged roast beef sandwich and a pint of chocolate milk and consumed them hungrily, sitting on the curb. The cab arrived. I told the driver's fat neck that I wanted to go to the Greyhound station. He nodded and drove. I pulled out my wallet and recounted my money. I knew how much it would cost for a return ticket, so I folded those bills and counted the rest, then watched the meter slowly approach that number. Five bucks away from my limit, we still seemed nowhere near where I needed to be. I cursed myself for buying food at the gas station. I wanted to tell the driver to stop, but found myself frozen and incapable. The amount on the meter reached my max, then started eating into my bus ticket money. Finally we reached the station. I paid the driver and had ten dollars left. Then I remembered you were supposed to tip cab drivers. I handed him the ten and asked for nine back. He rolled his eyes and told me to keep my money.

I approached the counter and explained where I needed to go and that I only had ten dollars. The lady wearing bifocals frowned and reiterated the price of the ticket, then said, "Next in line, please." I walked slowly to a seat by a vending machine and pounded my knee with my fist. I still had some change so I called Paul's house. One of his brothers answered and started dicking around when I asked if Paul was there, so I yelled at him. Paul picked up and said, "Oh, man, are you busted."

"What? Didn't you guys get my note?"

"Yeah, but your mom called and said she wanted to pick you up. Where are you? We've been driving around all day looking for you."

In the background Paul's mom said, "Is that Cedar? Where is he?"

"Paul, I need money. I need to get back home. I don't know what to do."

Noises on the phone rustled then Paul's mom spoke. "Cedar? Where are you? Your parents! Tell me where you are. We'll come get you."

I told Mrs. Dills where I was and added, "I don't have enough money to get back home." I gave her the phone number of the pay phone. She told me not to leave the station. I hung up and visited what appeared to be hell's restroom. The stalls were all locked and required a special token that cost twenty-five cents. Having just spent my last quarter, I did what it appeared every visitor to this lavatory did and pissed in the sink. That night I managed to catch some restless sleep on a bench under buzzing fluorescent fixtures. When I woke, it was morning and my sleep-deprived father was standing over me.

"Here's the deal," he said wearily, "you tell me everything, I'll tell you everything."

We had a six-hour drive ahead of us. The inside of the car was a shitty, sad place of food bags, empty soda cups, and newspapers. I drank coffee from a paper cup and ate a breakfast sandwich. My dad seemed too exhausted to bitch me out, reserving his energy for getting us back to the verdant edge of the state.

I retold the abortion story, this time with a new villain, George, making his malevolent appearance. I hoped to avoid punishment with my candor, but what exactly had I done that deserved punishment? I hadn't followed the prescribed routes of action that any adult would have counseled me to take, like talk to my parents, a psychiatrist, a cop. Instead, my actions had proceeded from theories about George, Jerry, and the loyalty of paternity. I told my father about Jerry showing up at the Greyhound station, *Rambo,* the pan of hot oil. Now would have been a good time for him to cross-examine me, but he stared at the road, nodding occasionally, saying nothing. I reminded myself that he'd heard worse tales than this. He conferred daily with drug dealers, arsonists, the fraudulent, and the scheming. I tried putting myself in his position, dealing with some tiresome bullshit about rescuing his kid from a bus station hundreds of miles from home. I expected at least an acknowledgement that my problems were worth sympathy. The more I could tell he didn't care, the more I became embarrassed at what was rolling out of my mouth.

When I was finished he said, "You done?"

"Yeah."

"My turn, then," he said, as though he had been waiting for me to shut up. "Your mom took pictures of me with another woman."

The inside of the car became like the heaving tissues of an internal organ, lined with sticky and diseased mucus. The blood in my head throbbed. He had nothing to say about my problems. A windshield-wiper blade captured a bug, its legs wriggling futiley as its yellow guts were squirted out of its thorax. My dad took another sip of his cold coffee.

"I saw the photos of you with that woman," I said.

"You jerked off onto a photo of that woman. Your mom thinks it was me."

"She'll believe me before she believes you."

"Whatever."

"Who is she?"

"Her name is Lorraine."

"How'd Mom get the pictures?"

"She took them from the parking garage across the street from the federal building."

"What does she do?"

"Look, Cedar, it doesn't really matter right now what she does or who she is."

"So, no one is really being up front. Except me."

"This will all have to be ironed out in court. I recommended a good divorce lawyer to your mom."

"That was nice of you."

"I should be really fucking mad at you right now, Cedar, but honestly, I don't have the energy for it."

"Don't you even see what kind of problems I'm dealing with?"

"Your bullshit is so miniscule compared to what I'm up against, let me tell you."

"What you're up against."

"You're going to hear contradictions coming from both sides. It's up to you to choose what to believe."

"Since when did we become sides?"

"I need to use the men's room. Rest stop ahead."

We pulled over at the rest area, where a roped-off patch of lawn designated for people to walk their dogs had been denuded of all flora by urine. Some pear-shaped World War II vets wearing their pointy hats sat behind a table set up with cookies, a coffee urn, and a sign that said DONA-TIONS GLADLY ACCEPTED. Their wives sat beside them, happily crafting sock puppets. I considered running into the woods while my dad peed, but he returned from the men's room before I could act on the impulse. I took a couple cookies and fed the remainder of my summer's earnings through the slit in the coffee can. We rode the rest of the way home in silence.

I still believed that both my parents wanted me, a belief that became harder to maintain when my dad deposited me at the house. Sleep deprivation had wrung any remnant of polite conversation out of my father. My running across the mountains seemed a massive inconvenience to everybody, almost as inconvenient as having to now punish me. There was a terse meeting of the three of us on the front porch, some language inserted in predictable places about trust and responsibility, and stern expressions. "I made you an appointment to see a counselor tomorrow," my mom concluded. The statement landed as an insult. Which of us needed a counselor? My parents exchanged some loveless logistical information and my dad got in his car and went to catch the ferry.

I found my room undisturbed, a histology book open on my desk where I'd left it, next to a plate that had once borne a corn dog, the stick adhered to a smear of blood-dark ketchup. I lifted my mattress and crawled underneath it. My mom came in and sat down on the end of my bed, on my foot.

"You must be hungry," she said.

"I'm okay," I said, my voice muffled.

"I need to tell you some things that will upset you."

"Like Dad cheated on you?"

"Yes. What did he tell you?"

"He knows you've been following them around like a detective."

"I suppose that's right."

"And that he jerked off onto that photo."

"I know it was you who did that to the photo."

Saying nothing, I admitted my guilt.

"When I met your father we had strong feelings about what was right and what was wrong. I worry that you lost your chance to feel that way. That no one's been there to help you sort it out."

"I'm sorry."

"It's not your fault. How's Kat?"

"I haven't talked to her since she punched me in the nose," I said.

"I came close to punching your father in the nose."

"How come you didn't?"

"Good question. He deserved it. Can you breathe under there?"

"No. I'm slowly suffocating."

"Before you die, can you promise me one thing?"

"Okay."

"Promise you'll come to me sooner next time something like Kat's situation happens?"

"Okay." It occurred to me that I might ask my mother how she was holding up. I imagined that she must have been feeling pretty bent up about my dad. But I held my concern, believing, stupidly, that to offer her comfort would have prevented her from providing comfort to me. She laid down on the bed, on the thick barrier between us, distributing her weight evenly along the length of my body and began to softly cry. I reached up from beneath the mattress, found her hand, and held it as I fell asleep.

The counselor worked in an office park surrounded by fir trees and the building reeked of antiseptics tarted up with artificial gardenias. His name was Mr. Cox and apparently he specialized in troubled teens. He shared the building with other boring businesses where boring people did boring-ass things. His Latino secretary led my mom and me to his shag-carpeted sanctum, more a living room than a place to shrink heads. He rose from a creaky swivel chair and pumped our arms in introduction, his handshake like a limp rag. His voice that of a sportscaster doing the play-by-play at a golf tournament. He wore a yellow polo shirt tucked into black-and-white checked slacks. Mr. Cox said he'd talk to me alone first, then to my mother, then to both of us together.

My mom left, announcing she had an errand to do. I sat down on the couch. A cigarette disintegrated in a nest of butts in an ashtray on the desk. Leaning back in his chair, Mr. Cox slid his fingers inside his waist band. The gesture would have been perverted if his pants hadn't wholly negated his sexuality.

"You can laugh at my name," Mr. Cox said. "Most people do."

"My friend has a cousin named Dick Dills," I said.

"That's good. I'm going to have to write that down in my little blue notebook." Then, apropos of nothing, he started to sing, "*Doe, a deer, a female deer. Ray, a drop of golden sun.* No? Not a fan of *The Sound of Music*? Well then, tell me, Cedar, what's on the other side of the mountains?"

"I'm not a runaway. I always meant to come back. I'm not like the other kids who come in here. I don't do drugs, I get good grades. I'm studying medical text books on my own because I'm going to be a doctor."

"And you needed to go on a little road trip to find someone."

"Yeah. I needed to find my—" I stopped. Mr. Cox didn't deserve to hear the real version. I suddenly understood that our transaction was no more important than one that occurred in the drive-through of a fast-food res-taurant. He expected to give me a particular kind of service in exchange for a certain kind of emotional currency. Then my mom could be billed for it.

I said, "I guess it was me I was trying to find."

"Did you in fact find yourself? Or did you come to be more lost?" Mr. Cox said.

"Why do you think you can help me?" I asked.

"I don't," Mr. Cox said. "In fact, I'm pretty sure your mother wasted fifty bucks sending you here. What makes you think I can help you?"

"I don't really."

"Then we're on equal footing, aren't we? See, Cedar, the simple fact is that because your family is relatively well off, and because you've maintained a reasonable level of academic achievement, you'll probably be just fine. I'll send you home with a couple brochures about a support group for kids of parents going through divorce and we'll call it even, how's that sound? You wouldn't believe the parents I get who drag their kids in here after catching them with a wine cooler. Ooooh, big crisis. They're beside themselves. Convinced their children are on the path to addiction. It doesn't really work that way, most of the time. The kids that really need help are the ones whose parents wouldn't ever consider sending them to a counselor." He started a new cigarette with the ember of his dying one. "You upper-middle-class kids will go off to college and have more-or-less healthy, heterosexual relationships, have careers, and produce children of your own that you'll send off to counselors after you catch them having sex or taking mushrooms. Meanwhile, I can make money off you people and afford to go in on a time-share on the Oregon coast and buy myself a snowmobile. Not that my own life is so great, when it boils down to it. My third wife just left me for a cosmetic surgeon, as a matter of fact. A guy who fixes noses and knockers, and right now I think they're in the Marshall Islands. Some fucking place where she sends me Polaroids of herself, topless, on a beach, with a mai tai in her hand, getting lotion rubbed on her tits by Frank's disembodied arm. Yeah, just happened a couple weeks ago, so you can tell I'm sorting through a few issues of my own. It's actually kind of refreshing to me that you find me full of shit, because that means I don't have to pretend I give a fuck. So, you ran away. Wow. No one's ever done that before. You must be the first teenager in history to pull off something like that."

"What are you going to tell my mom?"

"I'm going to tell her that you're the most brilliant goddamn fourteen-year-old I've ever met. That your grasp of the ethical dimensions of your actions is beyond what most *adults* are capable of. I'll throw in some reference to a study I read in a Danish mental-health journal about superadvanced levels of emotional intelligence in adolescents. It always impresses parents when I name-drop Piaget or Jung. How's that sound?"

True to his word, when my mother returned from her errands, Dr. Cox told her that I was one of—if not *the*—most gifted children he had ever worked with. "Mrs. Rivers, you can imagine the riffraff I get in here. Your son is a beam of light in the darkness of adolescence."

I was dismissed while my mom spoke to Mr. Cox alone, and spent ten minutes smugly flipping through the *Sports Illustrated* swimsuit issue. Years later my mother would tell me that Mr. Cox had explained that he'd tried to inflate my ego with praise and encourage me to imagine a better self. He told her that leveling with smarter kids and pretending he didn't care about their well-being sometimes elicited a level of trust from his young clients. By giving their self-image a little boost, often at his own expense, he provided them with an idealized template of themselves toward which they might slowly work. In other words, he'd tricked me into letting him help me.

Ever since we got it, our answering machine had featured the same awkwardly formal greeting. It was my father's voice, implying we simply weren't available, rather than not at home, to confuse would-be criminals who were calling ahead to determine whether it was safe to burglarize the place. My mother had changed the message in the past few days, recording a bland greeting in which she only acknowledged the phone number that had been called, naming none of the residents or former residents of the house. Hearing the new greeting crushed me, knowing that my dad's overly formal delivery, the same comfortable message that we'd had for three years, had been taped over forever.

When we returned home after my counseling session with Mr. Cox, I came in through the kitchen to find the answering machine recording and amplifying a call through its little speaker. It was Kat, quietly saying she needed to talk to me. Meanwhile, my mom dropped her purse on the floor and uttered a word or two of profanity. I was paying attention to Kat's message-in-progress as I crossed the room to pick up the phone, so it took me a moment to realize that somebody had broken into our house. As my hand settled on the receiver my mom said, "Wait." The plants on the end table had been knocked over, and were lying in piles of that weird dirt with the white pellets in it. The living room couch was absurdly upside-down, legs in the air. My mother said, "Don't touch anything. We need to leave." Kat hung up and the message machine started fast-forwarding and rewinding according to its own unfathomable logic.

Standing in the driveway, it took some effort to separate these two facts, our house getting trashed and Kat's message, as if they were tactile and auditory components of a singular loathing. My mom called 911 from her car phone. A short while later a cruiser pulled up and a female cop slowly walked toward us, uncapping a ballpoint with her teeth. She introduced herself as Officer Stoner, the best name for a cop I had ever heard. A statement was given. My father's name was intoned. While Officer Stoner put on latex gloves and dusted the place for fingerprints I crawled into my mom's car and called Kat. Veronica picked up, sounding far away. Kat picked up on another line and told her mom to hang up. We waited for the click.

"What happened? Why'd you call and leave that message?"

"I need to talk to you. Today. Can you meet me at Burger King in, like, an hour?"

"I don't know. Our house got broken into."

"What? Whatever, meet me in an hour."

I pushed the phone's antenna back into its orifice and punished myself by not cracking a window in the baking interior of the car. Officer Stoner came out of the house with my mom behind her. They motioned me to come over.

"What?" I said.

"We need you to show us your room and let us know if anything is missing," my mom said.

Inside, the sweaty residue of the intruder made the back of my neck itch. He'd been there and there, he'd seen this stuff over here, he had walked down this hall. I pushed open my bedroom door and saw that he had pulled up my mattress and thrown it against a wall. My porn mags were spread across the floor. My microscope was smashed—stomped on, apparently. But all my belongings seemed to be here, churned into disarray.

I leaned against the door frame and soberly told the officer there was nothing missing. I picked at a solidified paint drip on the bathroom door to keep from puking. My mother played the answering machine tape in the next room and we stood quietly as Kat's warbly message bounced around the house again.

"That's my girlfriend," I said. "Or she used to be."

"Do you have any reason to believe her message was in reference to what has happened to the house?" Officer Stoner inquired.

"She wouldn't do anything like this."

"We're just trying to narrow the possibilities," my mom said.

"Do you have any reason to believe this may have been done by your father?"

I was about to say no. I looked at some broken pottery, some *National Geographic*s ripped from their ordered, golden shelves, and thought of the time he threw his briefcase at the refrigerator. "I don't know," I said. Then, because I hated him, added, "maybe."

The officer asked a few more questions, then left. That was it? That was the extent of the crime-scene investigation? Didn't they want us to come down to the station and pore over dioramas of our house to recreate the intrusion? Later, we'd learn that the only fingerprints she had found were those belonging to our family. My father had an alibi formalized in court records of cases he had handled that day. Apparently, none of our belongings had been stolen, which meant the intruder had either not found what he was looking for or never intended to take anything in the first place. For days I'd feel on the verge of discovering something tangible that was missing, almost hoping to justify my sense that something irretrievable had been lost.

My mom announced we were staying in a hotel that night. She snatched a few pieces of clothing, a pillow, a jar of pickles, and her hair dryer. I stuffed a neurology text book and some underwear in my backpack. When I asked her if the hotel had a pool, she screamed, "Shut up! Just get in the car!" Back in the sedan the Talking Heads tape we'd been listening to fired up again as she turned the ignition. David Byrne's uncertain voice seemed the most inappropriate narrator one could ask for at a time like this, singing of architecture and memories that can't wait. My mom ejected the tape so hard it flew out of the deck and landed on the floor. I told her I had promised to meet Kat at Burger King. She didn't argue, being momentarily incapable of speech.

Finding myself alone at Burger King, I did what any sensible person in my situation would have done. I ordered a

Whopper. Except I had forgotten that I had no money left and so performed an embarrassing double take into my empty wallet at the counter, then shuffled off to loiter in the farthest corner of the restaurant. In this molded-plastic public zone I waited for Kat and read an abandoned sports page to pass the time. A couple kids without shoes screamed inside the playground equipment on the other side of the glass. I wondered how I'd ever considered such an environment fun. Kat finally showed up and set down her backpack.

"What happened?" I said.

"Why are you asking me?" Kat said, "You're the one who ran away from home. What was that about?"

"Paul told you?"

"No, Margot told me. Everyone knows about it. What did you think you were doing?"

"I went to see your dad."

Kat's face remained steady but the rest of her body gave her away. Her fingers made the strangest, crablike skitter across the table, a series of involuntary spasms possessing her hands. I grabbed hold of them and they were cold. She pulled them back, dragging her fingernails across the soft parts of my wrists.

"Oh my God you did not."

"I didn't see him for too long. I ran back to the bus station as quick as I could."

"But why did you go? What did you tell him?"

"I told him never to see you again."

"You what?" Kat yelled. A woman at the next table who looked like she'd stepped out of a *Far Side* cartoon tossed us a dirty look, her tongue still catching a drip from her vanilla cone. I suggested we go outside. In the playground I sat on a gigantic mushroom thing as Kat paced, arms crossed over her chest.

"You think you know everything about me. You think you can see inside my head. But you have no *clue* what I'm about. You barged into my life and started thinking you had authority over it. That thing that happened to me, I wish I'd never told you about it. I wish I'd just taken care of it by myself."

"I can't take this right now," I said. "Not after someone broke into my house."

"After someone broke into your stupid house? Cedar, my dad broke my fucking arm! He smashed it in a car door. He made me say it was an accident."

"Kat," I said, starting to cry, leaping to hold her but meeting her flailing arms.

"I never want to see you again," she muttered and hurried out through the gate, across the parking lot, onto her bike, and down the street.

This part is narrated
by Kat.

I. Hate. Boys. Their laughing big-toothed fucktard selves flicking orange pop from straws at pizza restaurants. Their grunts. The way they expect their moms to always wash their clothes. Their inability to make anything more complicated than a cheese sandwich. The cock rock they blast into their heads through scuzzy earphones; the ugly, guitar-playing thirty-year-old men in spandex pants with long hair that they worship. Their pathetically obsessive creation of fantasy worlds using dice that have more than six sides. Their phony professional wrestling, staged by other idols in spandex pants. Their drawings of skulls, over and over and over, with a ballpoint pen, on sheets of college-ruled paper. That they call these drawings art. Their skateboards (no, actually, I kind of like those). Wedgies and swirlies. The way they blow their noses by pushing one nostril closed then exhaling sharply through the other nostril, spraying a projectile they call a "snot rocket." The way they pretend to be sensitive by writing hideous poetry. The unused condoms petrified in their wallets. *Monty Python* skit recitations. Belching contests. Memorized sports statistics; the hypothetical matchups between players and teams. Auto shop. Their pip-squeak mustaches. The ease with which they deliver a crippling insult. Their stinking feet. The way they try to show off on the high dive. The slow creep of a clammy hand across your leg in a movie theater. The religious fervor of blow job procurement.

Boxing. The sanctimonious way they say "you should read this" while standing next to you in a bookstore. Their lecturing manner when talking about music. How they assume you don't know anything about Stanley Kubrick. Beer and beer and beer. How they trash their own dorm then hang out at yours all the time because you actually take the time to clean it and avoid such phenomena as rotting turkey carcasses, taking up sink space. The unwarranted aggressiveness with which they play Frisbee. The way, exuding a stench of martyrdom, they confide it just doesn't feel the same with a condom. The loudness with which they eat. Their laissez-faire hygiene, particularly dental. Cigars! Expensive stereo equipment in an un-feng-shui'ed living room. The assumption that you don't know how to manage your money. Lectures about Miles Davis and Bob Dylan. Military history. The disproportionate pride they exhibit after having changed a tire.

Their other girlfriend. The bounced checks they try to cover up. The subscription to the idiotic magazine with the enhanced women on the cover that—pathetically, really—doesn't even have the balls to really qualify as pornography. The sight of them reading advice columns from this magazine while eating Grape-Nuts. Motorcycles. The big deal they make about actually running the vacuum cleaner. Their rudeness with sales people. Their inability to buy a decent present for their parents without your input.

Their wars, their sexual assaults, their invented chemicals in rivers and bloodstreams. Male gynecologists. Their odious opinions broadcast on talk radio. Their seemingly unimpeachable authority on how professional athletes and their managers should have conducted themselves in any number of situations. Their angry voices, ending arguments with the sheer advantage of volume. Their inability to admit a mistake. Their ear hair. Their guns. The righteousness of yard maintenance. The time they lied about paying for the car registration. That they assume you don't know anything about computers. Their opinions on how entire countries and civilizations should conduct themselves, and their perplexity that these opinions are not publicly praised and immediately codified into law. Their sagging bellies. When they say precisely the wrong thing at the wrong time to their children. Shaving cuts. Auto parts. The volume of their disappointments and regrets.

How I love them!

Misconception

* * *

George knocks softly, comes into my room, and smooths a corner of my bed to sit on. "You wanna talk?" he says. The only possible answer is no. I choose not to say anything and stare at the binder my mother bought me for school, the powder blue one with the word *Malibu* on the front. I'm not sure if Malibu is in California or Florida, and whether the airbrushed image is of the Pacific or Atlantic. Either way it looks preferable to the barnacle-encrusted bouldery beaches of Puget Sound.

At the mall I have taken note of all the surf-themed T-shirts worn by kids who have just come in out of the rain—the pictures of lazily leaning surfers or the words "Official Bikini Inspector" sticking to the boys' skinny chests. I wonder if kids in Hawaii wear shirts with decals of logging trucks and spawning salmon on them. The brands I have allegiance to declare themeselves in 250-point type across the front of my expanding breasts. I'm wearing one now. Esprit.

"I had to move around a lot as a kid, too," George says. "I know how it can be. Omaha, Lincoln, then over to Reno, Boise. A new school every year for a while. But you'll get to go to the same school, so that's good."

"What do you even want?" I say.

George smirks and says, "To tell you the truth, what I really want is ice cream. You up for a treat?"

George drives a powder blue Monte Carlo with an 8-track player and a scented tree. Between the two front seats is a padded console he bought at an auto-supply store, in which he stashes Kleenex, a pad and pen, a mug with a brown crescent of dried Sanka in the bottom, and 8-track cassettes of Tony Orlando and Dawn, the Carpenters, Kenny Rogers, Neil Diamond, and Captain and Tennille, the greatest hits of whom is currently inserted in the deck. Who were they trying to fool? Captain and Tennille only ever really had one hit: "Love Will Keep Us Together." They could have released it on a 45 and called the record "Greatest Hits." I secretly love that song, though, and don't object when it comes on. George taps his thick and ugly class ring against the steering wheel and sings along to the "I will! I will! I will!" chorus. I avert my eyes out the rainy window and unfocus them until all I see is blur.

At Big Scoop George says I can order anything I want, within reason. I scan the menu looking for the most un-reasonable item. The triple-dip cone? Pretty reasonable. Banana split? Borderline reasonable. I suppose he means those big party parfaits that serve ten five-year-olds ("or five hungry grown-ups!"). These and other mystical con-fections glow weakly from the washed-out, translucent plastic sheets taped to the lighted menu board. No one who orders them expects the teens who work here to cre-ate exact replicas. I select a sundae with two scoops and caramel sauce, and George nods as if to approve of my restraint. He orders the most asinine treat here: a frozen banana on a stick, dipped in chocolate and rolled in smashed peanut bits. I have never seen this item consumed at this place and always thought it was the confectionery world's equivalent to parsley—something to observe but not actually eat.

We sit near a window that looks out on the pit of a lube, oil, and filter place. George cracks his knuckles in the most grotesque manner possible, with a couple knuckles squealing as they pop.

George says, "I know I'm going to get arthritis from doing this but what the heck, you only live once."

"Thanks for the ice cream," I say, and his face brightens like it's the kindest thing anyone has said to him all week.

"Well it's my pleasure," George says. "I hope we can have more of these kinds of outings."

I shrug, swirling molten caramel around a long-necked spoon.

"You don't go for the nuts on your sundae, is that your story?" George asks.

"I hate peanuts," I say.

"Well, then, I won't offer you a bite of this here banana."

"I don't know why you ordered that. We're in an ice-cream parlor. Don't you think you should at least order ice cream at an ice-cream parlor?"

George shrugs. "Gives me gas, usually," he says, "and I forgot to bring my Beano."

"This conversation is fantastic," I say.

"What do girls like to talk about?" George asks, apparently nonrhetorically. "Boys, right? What about this boyfriend of yours, Tree?"

"His name is Cedar."

"Is he an Indian?"

"You mean Native American?"

"I guess he doesn't look like an Indian. Where'd he get the funny tree name?"

"I don't know? His parents maybe?"

"Must have been high on dope when they named him. Hey, did you mention he mows lawns? I'm thinking that with my back acting up like it has been I should hand over the reins to someone new. Does he know how to use a weed whacker?"

"He's really good at whacking," I say.

"You can ask him for me, the next time you see him."

"We broke up. I'm not seeing him anymore."

"Broke up! No wonder you've been in such a crumb-bum mood. I tell you, getting dumped is the pits. I remember that sensation all too well."

"It was me who dumped him."

"Oh, you were the dumper. Can't say I've ever been on that end of the equation." George looks to his banana for some sort of wisdom that isn't forthcoming. "But I wanted to ask you, do you think—does your mom ever talk about me?"

"About you? Only when she's insulting your driving."

"I'm serious," George says. There's a nugget of peanut on his chin. I let it stay there. He continues, "Because I want to make sure she doesn't feel like she's just settling."

"Why would she think that?" I ask.

George looks down the front of his body, half laughs at his own expense, then squints out the window. "Look at me, Kat. Do I look like the kind of man who gets a lot of attention from women? I couldn't believe it when your mom agreed to go on a date with me. I thought the whole time we were out to dinner that the hidden cameras were going to come out and I'd be exposed for the chump I am. I want her to know that I'm up for the task, that I intend to be a really good man for her."

"Okay," I say.

"And part of it, well, part of me doing right by her means doing right by you. It's got to be strange for you to have this bald, weird guy show up one day and start hanging around with your mom all the time. You and her are so close; it's a special thing, sure. Now she's paying less attention to you, that's got to be hard. But I hope that if you see I can make your mom happy, you'll be happy for her, and maybe let me be a little part of your life, too."

I'm like a little squirrel, sniffing at a piece of food from the hand of someone who wants my trust. I don't know what I'm supposed to do. My sundae is melting and my hand has somehow fallen asleep. The words *My dad* leave my mouth and fall into the conversation and don't move. George just listens.

"My dad used to hurt me," I say.

"I know, Katie."

"I don't need anything from you about this. That's not why I'm telling you. You just need to know something for your own good. My mom and I made a pact to kill anyone who hurts me like that again. I'm serious."

We watch the men changing the oil on a Dodge pickup truck. George squints, thinking, then says, "I'm sure my daughter wants to kill me."

"Where does she live?"

"I have no idea. She was in Louisiana last I knew. That was five years ago. No, six."

"What's she do?"

"She's a full-time drug addict."

"What about her mom?"

"Her mom has her own problems. I haven't talked to her in eight years, since she kicked me out."

"She dumped you?"

"This wasn't what you'd call getting dumped. This was my family dismantling itself before my eyes. In movies people throw dishes at the walls, and we actually did. So I moved out here to get a fresh start."

From outside came the sound of a pneumatic wrench freeing a tire of lug nuts.

Misconception

"You ever hear the story about Johnny Cash and the cave?" George asked. "You know who Johnny Cash is, right?"

"The country guy?"

"Yeah. Well, he was messed up on dope pretty bad at one point, hated his life, didn't get along with his wife June, just wanted to die."

"What's Johnny Cash have to do with you moving out here?"

"Everything. So Cash goes out in the woods in Tennessee where there was a big cave. Kind of like the one in *Tom Sawyer* where Tom and Becky get lost. Deep and long and vast. A place where Indians used to live. He gets down on his belly and crawls into that cave and decides he isn't going to crawl out. He keeps going and going, for miles it seems, and his flashlight eventually goes out and he's down there ready to die. He gives up. Throws in the towel. Then he feels the presence of the Lord. And the Lord tells Johnny that He wants him to *live*. So Johnny starts crawling back, even though he has no idea where he's supposed to be going. He just crawls and crawls and he knows he isn't meant to die just yet, he knows he has more to give to the world. So when he finally comes back out, who does he see standing there?"

"Jesus?" I say.

"No, smart aleck, he sees the woman he loves. June. Waiting for him with a big basket of food."

"What happened then?"

"That's the end of the story. Well, I guess he got his TV show after that, but my point is that these past couple months maybe I've felt a little like Johnny Cash when he crawled out of that cave. Coming out of a dark place with a family waiting for me on the other side."

I don't want George's kindness to leave me, as much as I pretend to despise him. We finish our treats and I follow him back to his car, where he cranks the heat on this unseasonably cold night and shoves another 8-track into the deck.

My mother is freaking out. She's trying on her dress, pivoting in front of her new bedroom mirror in her new walk-in closet that's still somewhat of a novelty. The wedding dress has the power to make my mother regress in age some thirty years. She's asking if it looks like her arm fat is hanging down. She talks about the need to get a loofah for her back so it won't be zitty on wedding day, because she never has her back exposed like this, and does the color make her look ridiculous? She thinks the seashell pink is kind of classy, not disingenuous like white would have been. Gloves? On or off? Veil, what do you think about the veil? She's pivoting left, surveying her ass, trying to do the impossible by imagining her ass as seen from behind while only able to see it in profile. "Get another mirror," she says, so I obediently fetch a hand mirror and hold it up while she assumes a sort of squat position, like she's auditioning for the role of the Hunchback of Notre Dame, asking if her ass looks wide.

"Are you planning to walk down the aisle that way?" I ask.

"I'm serious! What if I have to bend down and pick up something that I dropped?"

I sit on the corner of the bed and retie my shoe. "When did you get like this? Who cares? You look fine. God!"

"Quit with the attitude. I need your help. You haven't even showed me what you look like in your dress."

"I told you it's fine. I just don't want to wear it for longer than absolutely necessary."

"You never liked dresses. What a luxury for you. When I was in school I didn't have a choice about dresses. It was either dresses or skirts."

"When you were in school—" I start to say something sarcastic but suddenly my mother's face is gobbed up and preparing to cry. Her hands fly up to the sides of her face as if to wrestle it back into a calm expression, then out comes a sob, so forceful I don't know what I'm supposed to do about it.

"Kat, why didn't you tell me?"

"Tell you what, Mom?"

My mother slowly opens her jewelry box, removes the pregnancy test, and sets it in my hand. She's sitting next to me, the substandard mattress of the king-size bed sagging in the middle.

"You're supposed to *tell* me these things, Kat," she says. The sentence doesn't sound like me getting in trouble. It sounds like my mother needing something from me. "We're a team," she says.

"I didn't want to mess up your wedding."

She checks her makeup to see if it's becoming a disaster. "My wedding," she says. "Hand me a tissue, will you?"

I pull a Kleenex out of a box that is itself contained in a box called a *cozy*.

"When did you get the abortion?" she asks.

"What?"

My mother stands and pivots in her wedding dress, tears welling at the edges of her eyes. "Don't, don't, *don't*. I need you to not pretend right now. I need you to tell me the truth or, so help me. I found this test a month ago. I've seen your tampon wrappers in the bathroom trash since then."

"You knew I was pregnant a month ago?"

"I found it when we were moving."

"Why didn't you say something then?" I say, crying now, though it takes me a second to figure out why. "You could have helped me, Mom."

"I didn't want to believe it, and then everything with George happened. We were getting along really well."

"So I was right that you shouldn't have known."

This woman named Veronica who is my mom, on the verge of getting married, grabs my arms and digs her artificial nails into the soft skin. I can't tell if she's trying to hold me or throw me against the wall. "You should have told me. And I should have talked to you about it. We both fucked up, all right? What am I supposed to do? Do we get back in the car and go somewhere else, get a new job, start you at a new school? Do I marry this guy?"

"Does he love you?"

"I think he does."

"Then do it, Mom."

"I want you to be my little girl."

I'm wearing faded jeans and a zippered sweatshirt. Socks with holes in them and fingernails painted black with permanent marker. I'm looking at my mother and myself in the closet mirror and it's a perplexing reversal, me in frayed, worn clothes, my mother crying, wrapped in taffeta and lace. She sits back down on the bed and sniffs tears into her throat. She says, "George can't know this. You can never tell him."

"Why?"

"Listen to me, Kat. George has certain beliefs, certain ways of thinking that might not let him understand why you did what you did."

"What would happen if I told him?"

My mother pauses a beat. "That's not going to happen, Kat."

"You don't even seem to care about what happened to me."

She rises from the bed and consults a row of perfume bottles on the dresser. Choosing one with a tall, thin vaporizer she sprays it up into the air, letting the atomized haze of scent settle into her hair. "I do care, Kat," she says, "because I know how hard your decision was. I came close to getting an abortion myself once."

I am still thinking about George. "If I told him what happened, do you think he wouldn't marry you?"

"I think he'd make me choose between him and you. I don't think he'd let you live under this roof."

"And what would you choose?"

"This isn't fair, Katie. My wedding, all the house stuff, why did you choose to pull all this crap on me right now?"

"What would you choose?"

"He's got *money*. You know how happy I'm going to be when I can just have one part-time job? Do you realize how much you-and-me time that's going to free up? We've been waiting for something like this for a long time. Jesus, Kat, you could go to *college*."

"You'd choose him."

"I'd do what I always do and choose what is best for both of us."

"You don't want him to know, because you'd be ashamed of me."

Misconception

"I'm not ashamed of you."

"Then why do I have to hide this thing that happened?"

"I know how hard this is for you."

"How? You know shit about what it's like for me."

"I know," she says, "because I came close to aborting you."

Santa Cruz, 1970.

Veronica climbed naked from the ocean. Scaly clouds kept the air gray and quiet except for the distant calls of sea lions. In the sand about twenty yards from a little peeled-paint green shack was a mattress covered with a floral-print fitted sheet. She couldn't remember how it had gotten out there or whose idea it had been. Whether it had happened last night or the night before. There were smears of sand on it, a footprint. But most conspicuously, dressed in blue jeans and nothing else, was Jerry, asleep on it. Still dripping from her swim, Veronica stood over him. Saltwater slid down her body and found its channels between her breasts, down her belly, collecting in the hair between her legs. She waited quietly for Jerry to wake up, knowing he would sense her and rise from his dream. He turned over on his back. Sunlight briefly split a cloud about a quarter mile off shore, sending a shaft into the water.

"Who are you?" Jerry said.

"I'm the one you shared this mattress with last night."

"Oh yeah."

"You do realize you're sleeping on a beach."

"I realize you're making it hard for me to sleep."

"Come on. Let's go get some breakfast."

Jerry pulled himself up onto his elbows. "I don't know about you, but I was just planning on ordering room service."

Veronica laughed and settled onto the gritty mattress. "I'm serious. Where did you come from?"

"San Diego or thereabouts. It's early."

"I won't embarrass you and make you admit you don't know my name. I'm Veronica."

"I'm Jerry. Nice to meet you."

These two people who'd been balling ten hours before shook hands. Jerry found his sandals and shook out the sand. They pulled the mattress back to the flaky green house and set it sagging against the outside wall. Inside, the others weren't yet awake. They slept in sleeping bags or wrapped in threadbare blankets. In the bedroom, a bed frame outlined three people curled together on the floor below where the mattress should have been. Jerry went to the kitchen, looking for food while Veronica put her clothes back on. Empty bottles crowded the counters. The refrigerator held little other than a copy of *Life* magazine and a jar of gefilte fish.

"You got any bread?" Jerry asked.

"Like, to make a sandwich?"

"That kind of bread would be good, too."

"I know a good pancake stand in town. They won't hassle us."

"Pancakes," Jerry said. "Okay."

Out behind the house they rediscovered their vehicles—his a Chevy truck, hers a Beetle. Both happened to be painted the same baby blue. The back of Jerry's truck was covered with a green army-surplus tarp that he pulled back to expose a mess of auto parts, beer boxes, clothes, plywood, and stuff salvaged from the beach. From a backpack he yanked a wadded T-shirt with a message on it: *I Smoked Dope and All I Got Was Stoned.* He found a flannel shirt and put that on, too.

"You like driving around with all that stuff in your truck?" Veronica said.

"You see crapola in there, I see a living. You wouldn't believe what some guys are willing to pay for these parts."

"Parts of what?"

"Expensive cars. I got a knack for finding things that other folks don't realize are valuable."

"Is that what you're doing in Santa Cruz?"

"To tell you the truth, I have no clue what the hell I'm doing in Santa Cruz."

Veronica got into the truck. This guy's scent filled the cab. Funny how body smells, traded back and forth through sex, became intensified when the other person wears them. Veronica tried unsuccessfully to remember if Jerry had worn a rubber the night before. Jerry was pretty sure he hadn't. He remembered the surf, rolling in high enough to touch the bottom edge of the mattress, thinking how groovy it would be if they were washed to sea, the mattress their raft. But tides recede and people wake up to find themselves tragically sober, hungry, and resolutely not horny. Jerry looked at his watch but even though it told him what time it was, it didn't really mean that much to him.

The pancake stand sold pancakes on paper plates and you could walk around on the beach, eating them. Jerry ordered a short stack and Veronica ordered a cinnamon roll. They sat on a concrete abutment watching the surf. Jerry burned the roof of his mouth with the coffee. Veronica ate her pastry counterclockwise.

"How do you know Jonas and Caroline?" Veronica said.

"I know a Jonas and Caroline?"

"The folks whose pad we partied at last night."

"I don't know them. Some guy at a bar told me about the party and I went along. I only just got here yesterday. You live here?"

"San Fran," Veronica said. "I was visiting a friend."

"Where's the friend?"

"Beats me. She wasn't in town when I arrived. Are you passing through or setting up here?"

"I got a job up north, rebuilding tractors, eventually. My uncle set me up with this one guy, does jobs for all the apple farmers up there. Fixing manure spreaders. Stuff like that." Jerry wanted to slap his forehead. Manure spreaders? A chick like this is going to dig farm machinery? He stared into the swirling cream tornado of his coffee. Man, you roll into town, ask a dude at the first bar you set foot in where to score some grass, end up three sheets to the wind at a house party where they're playing the same damn Electric Flag album all night, pass out, and wake up on a mattress on the beach with a gorgeous blonde standing naked over you. What heaven was this? Even the coffee was good. Probably the best he'd ever had. And now look, the day was unfurling over the beach downright cinematically. The clouds were departing, taking his hangover with them. He had a truck load of Stutz Bearcat parts some lawyer in Eureka was willing to pay five hundred for, which would be more than enough to get up north and settle into his job as a shit spreader repair man. Problem was getting from Santa Cruz to Eureka. Fifteen bucks wasn't going to put a whole lot of gas in the tank, especially not after he spent another fifty cents of it on one of those delicious-looking cinnamon rolls. *Holy shit,* Jerry thought, *my cock! It was inside this girl last night!*

"I was just joking about the manure spreader," he said.

"Sure you were," Veronica said.

"Why do I feel like I know you?" Jerry said.

"I look like a lot of people."

"You look like no one I've ever known."

"You ever watch TV?"

"You're an actress?"

"Not really. Ever see the *Pop Hour*?"

"Sure. That still on the air?"

"It was until a couple years ago. I was a featured dancer."

"No kidding. I must of seen you a hundred times."

"Probably not. I was only in eighty-seven episodes. Anyway, after that I moved to Frisco. Scene's really gotten to be a drag there, though. They take these tour buses to the Haight for fat tourists to laugh at the hippies. I got out a month ago after a boy got shot in front of my apartment."

"So you're not just visiting Santa Cruz?"

"I call it visiting if you don't have a place of your own."

"Did I already ask if you had any bread?"

"I don't. But I know how to get some." Veronica looked into her coffee and thought, *I'm doing this. Here's a guy with four days of facial hair growth, grime under his fingernails, and a car full of probably stolen auto parts. Here's a guy who I want to leap into the arms of.* The stupidity of the idea was precisely what made it so appealing. *I will finally escape California,* Veronica thought. A farm. This guy was heading to a farm. Maybe there would be orchards, and barns, and goats.

Back at the green beach house the residents had begun to stir. Some cat was preparing water for oolong tea over the barbecue pit while the spitting image of Mama Cass played an ocarina. Everyone's eyes were like doors that had gotten kicked open by cops the night before. Veronica showed Jerry to her car and opened the trunk in the front. Inside were clothes, mostly, some paperbacks, and a tire iron. She dug around a while, churning floral-print fabrics.

"It's not here," she said. "I had a brick of dope."

"What do you mean a brick?"

"A kilo. I was selling it bit by bit to pay for stuff. God-damn it!"

"You sure we didn't smoke it last night?"

"We'd all be dead of smoke inhalation if we did. I'm sure it was here. I'm positive." Veronica kicked her bumper and tromped into the house with Jerry close behind. "Any-one seen Jonas? Where the hell's Jonas?"

A chick named Mimi pointed in the direction of the beach. Jonas was catching some surf, she said. Soon Veronica was standing on the shore, yelling Jonas's name at the dis-tant figures riding the waves. After a while Jonas wiped out and trudged with his board up the sand.

"You stole my brick," Veronica said.

"Wha?" Jonas's hair dripped in front of his face. He flung it back and squinched up his eyes. Either the salt-water was getting to him or he was seriously baked. "I don't know what you're talking about, sister."

"Her dope, asshole," Jerry said. "Her kilo of weed."

"I didn't do nothing with your brick of weed," he said, scratching his balls, moving toward the house.

"Look, man, that dope is what she's been living off of. Be a good brother and give it back," said Jerry.

"I said I didn't fuckin' take your weed!" Jonas shouted over his shoulder, ducking through the sliding door, wiping aside the vertical blinds. Veronica started to follow. Jerry grabbed her elbow.

"No, you go get in my truck. I'll take care of this."

"It's my grass, I'll deal with it," Veronica said.

Jerry pressed the keys to his truck into her hand. "I ain't joking, woman. Wait in the truck."

Veronica gave in, went around back past the mattress, which already had a new sleeper, and climbed into the Chevy to sulk. She tried the glove compartment but found it locked. Behind the seat were a few issues of *Playboy*. She started reading an interview with Jean Paul Sartre. About halfway through, Jerry startled her, tapping at the window.

"Get your shit," he said. "We gotta move." Jerry's lip was fat. Speckles of blood dotted his T-shirt.

"What did you do to him?"

"I got your dope back," Jerry said, thrusting a paper bag at her. "I'm serious. Get your fucking stuff *now*."

When she didn't move, Jerry started grabbing arm loads of Veronica's belongings from her car and dumping them in the back of his truck.

"What the hell? Where are we going?"

A kid with no shirt, thick glasses, and a skinny headband burst from the house and started yelling. "You think you can just get away with shit like that, man? Well you're fucked. You know that? This is a loving household, man. We don't grok that kind of antisocial behavior here."

By now Jerry had emptied the Beetle of Veronica's worldly and weirdly goods and climbed into the driver's seat. Others started trickling out of the house, shuffling nonconfrontationally in the gravel. Jerry gunned the engine. "Flower child rule number one," he yelled, "don't bogart the fuckin' dope." They sped away, churning up dust. Veronica watched the kid with glasses yelling with both hands configured in middle fingers.

"We're heading north. You and me," Jerry said. "How's that sound?"

"What about my car?" Veronica said.

"Your car was a piece of shit. I'll steal you a new one."

After selling the auto parts to the gay lawyer in Eureka, for a lot less than originally quoted, Jerry and Veronica entered that part of California that is less about the ocean than it is about the ancient trees. Veronica rode with her elbow on the window frame, hand keeping the wind from whipping her eyes with strands of her long hair. Jerry's pheromones filled the truck, shuffling Veronica's thoughts: an animal asking a hunter for forgiveness, a mountain to be climbed, some waitress's phone number written inside a matchbook cover, swirling galaxies. They pulled off the road, climbed through the trees for a few yards, and made love on the cool forest floor. Later, a can of Schlitz beer rolled around on the passenger-side floor. They picked up a trio of Indian teenagers hitchhiking north and got them high for free. Jerry checked the rearview whenever there was a chance the fuzz might be on their tail, which seemed to be every two minutes. Then Oregon happened. Up the coast, through little towns, to their left Asia, to their right the heartland. Jerry pitched his tent on a bluff overlooking the surf.

"Let's stop here for good," Veronica said, "let's live here."

But Jerry kissed her and said "No babe, we got good things waiting for us up in *Warsh*ington."

The morning Veronica decided she was in love with this guy it rained. They walked naked on the beach anyway, throwing a piece of worm-eaten driftwood for a stray dog, standing in the surf. These days felt wrongly ordered, starting with a conception, then their introduction on the beach, then a honeymoon up the coast. Veronica sat in a state park restroom stall crying, gazing at what was definitely not a period in the panties. She considered roaming the campground asking randomly selected vacationers, *Excuse me, have you seen my period? I seem to have lost it. What's it look like? Uh, kinda heavy, bloody? I was supposed to have it by now?* Back in the tent Jerry, oblivious, rolled himself another spliff and dug a book on what it meant to be a Capricorn.

I don't even know this guy, Veronica thought. Then she thought, *This is how it's supposed to happen, though. This is the part where I decide to get married.*

They turned eastward and drove across the Cascades, into scrub pines and furrowed beige hills. Veronica immediately missed the irrational border of ocean waves. Inland was where they were headed. Today bore the sorrows of a Sunday even though it was Wednesday. For hundreds of miles Jerry fiddled with the radio, following news reports of a gruesome triple homicide and fierce debates about the new abortion law, Referendum 20. A fourteen-year-old kid had stabbed his parents and older sister while they slept, then arranged their bodies as though they were kneeling in prayer at their bedsides. For two weeks he continued attending school, getting straight As on his tests, going to wrestling practice, even showing up at a dance. His sister's college noticed she hadn't checked in with the registrar to sign up for fall classes, made some phone calls, and eventually the police showed up at the house and found the kid eating a bowl of cereal in front of a rerun of *The Andy Griffith Show*. Veronica leaned out the window and vomited loudly. News radio provided ample cover for morning sickness.

They pulled into the farm in the late afternoon. The place didn't look like much: three buildings and a house, a dozen sheep in a pen. But surrounding the house were rows of beautiful apple trees rising and falling on the hills. Jerry's knock on the screen door went unanswered, but a minute later an old farmer appeared in blue coveralls, cleaning a piece of machinery with an ex-undershirt.

"I'm here about the mechanic job," Jerry said.

"Mechanic job." The farmer echoed, sort of observing the words as they hung in the air. "Mechanic job," he repeated.

"Yeah, my uncle . . ." As Jerry explained, Veronica watched the farmer's empathetic face and knew there was no job to be had.

Back in the truck, Jerry let his hands dangle limply over the steering wheel. "My uncle Russ promised me there was a job here."

"This is probably a bad time to tell you I'm pregnant," Veronica said.

The wedding,
narrated by Cedar.

I hung out by the Saint Matthew's playground as cars rolled into the crunchy gravel parking lot bearing generations in formal wear. I had been added to the guest list as something of an anomaly, related to no one, no one's friend, too young to partake of the open bar. A black Lincoln Continental performed an excruciating routine of jettisoning old people sweating in blazers, sausage bodies stuffed into dresses and painful shoes. There were purses and flowers and camera bags to gather, hair to be checked, nieces and nephews to castigate for not hewing to the expectations on how weddings were supposed to proceed. I wore a white shirt and my only tie, which was made of black leather and measured about a half inch wide. My mom had told me I was expected to arrive with a gift and had given me twenty dollars to buy a picture frame, for which I had paid extra to have wrapped in Maps of the

World wrapping paper. More cars arrived, a clump of them, and from one emerged the bride, surrounded by a couple of cackling women I'd later learn were Veronica's sisters, in matching pink dresses. In this gaggle of baby's breath and severely teased hair was Kat, packaged in a white dress. I wanted to run. She saw me and came over.

"You came," Kat said.

"I got your mom a present."

"You didn't have to come."

"I'll go if you want me to."

"That's not what I meant. I did want you to come. I just thought you wouldn't."

"I don't know anybody here."

Kat pointed across the parking lot. "That's my uncle Vernon. He's with his wife Jo Anne. He's been married three times. He's completely rich. You know that little plastic dealie that makes it so the cheese doesn't stick to the pizza box? He invented that."

"Who's the guy in the wheelchair?"

"I don't know. I think he's a friend of George's."

"You probably need to go inside," I said.

"Yeah, but come with me," Kat said, taking my hand, leading me into the church. At the door, three manicured women doused with perfume applied boutonnieres to the tuxes of three boozy men. Groomsmen. One of them chucked Kat on the shoulder and said, "Hey little lady. Ready to see your mom get hitched?"

"Hi Uncle Al," Kat said.

"Who's your friend?" Uncle Al asked.

"This is my boyfriend, Cedar."

Boyfriend!

One of the boutonniere appliers said, "You'd better get in there, Kat. Your mom is looking for you," and Kat pried her fingers slowly from mine, then hurried into a bridal preparation sanctum. I wandered into the vast church. Slowly the pews filled with people, conversation, and bored kids fiddling with the golf pencils and weekly missals. A seemingly mentally disabled organist played a few hymns, leaning close to the sheet music to better read it through her thick glasses, bobbing her head perhaps more emotionally than the occasion required. A man with slicked-back hair walked down the aisle looking for a seat, a length of toilet paper trailing from the waistband of his plaid slacks. The young couple behind me engaged in a hushed argument. A thick woman in a purple dress scooted into the pew beside me and introduced herself as Loretta Root.

"I'm Cedar. I'm the maid of honor's boyfriend."

"Well she looks quite sweet today. You're a lucky young man. And just let me know if you need a tissue; I brought extras. I can't hardly make it through these things without turning on the waterworks. You here with anyone?"

"No."

"Me neither. Looks like I found me a date."

"How do you know the bride and groom?" I asked.

"Old George volunteers at the soup kitchen I manage. Usually mans the sandwich table. Makes a mean PB and J."

Then the wedding commenced. We rose. Barely five minutes into the ceremony Loretta Root's waterworks kicked in, rendering the travel-size packet of Kleenex she retrieved from her purse frighteningly insufficient. As the priest spoke about holy bonds and God's grace, Ms. Root honked into her toiletries and at one point grabbed tightly onto my hand. She dug into her purse and pulled out a studio portrait of a little boy, who could have been a grandson, to which she spoke in a low whisper between sobs. We rose and sang hymns, Loretta pointing out how to return to the chorus at the end of a new verse. In the music and singing and invocations of love, I felt the summer's layers of hurt stripped from my conscience. The bride and groom kissed. Loretta gave me a big hug, smashing my face between a set of immortal tits.

Free food and beverages awaited a few blocks away at All-Purpose Hall. I would pull Kat close and slow dance with her and everyone would know we were in love. After the rice tossing, I caught a ride in Loretta's Taurus, which had the air conditioning set to max and three vanilla-roma trees swinging from the rearview. Yanking a gigantic wrapped present from the trunk of her car when we arrived, she said, "You go on and find your young lady friend. I'm sure she wants to see you."

Tonight the All-Purpose Hall's purpose was that of a disco, with a mirror ball, streamers, and tables with punch and hors d'oeuvres, an assemblage that one aged man loudly dubbed "the whole nine yards!"

I occupied my hands with a plastic cup of punch and sat in a fold-out chair in a corner in anticipation of the wedding party. When they finally arrived, they formed a receiving line and the guests slowly hugged and kissed their way through the gauntlet of newlyweds. Flashes popped and Polaroid cameras spit out their square, ripening frames. Little nieces and nephews took turns pretending to be John Travolta: pointing skyward, then to the dance floor, then skyward once more. I joined the receiving line. When I reached the bride and groom, Veronica hugged me and told me how special it was that I had come. My shoulders tensed as George clapped me on the back and laughed and advised not to spike the punch. Then Kat threw her arms around my neck and we hugged for a long time. "Everything is good," she said, and for another half hour no one could have convinced me otherwise.

A band appeared: four gentlemen in matching tuxes with blue glitter ties and cummerbunds and a woman singer in a gold lamé' dress and football-grade shoulder pads. The lights dimmed and the All-Purpose Hall assumed the ambience of a high school prom. George and Veronica danced to a Peter Cetera song. I overheard one of the guests observe that the sax player was as good as Kenny G. As soon as the dance concluded in a kiss and applause, the amplified kick drum thudded and the singer snarled into the microphone. "*Left a good job in the citah, workinferthe-man every night and day, heh! Come on now let's see some of you out on the dance floor. Grandad over there, why don't you show these kids how to get funky! Hey! Rollin' on the riverrrrrr.*"

Kat kicked off her shoes, slid over to me in her stockings, and grabbed my hand. "We have to dance!"

"I don't know how!" I said, which was true. Dancing made little sense to me and I found myself overthinking what to do next. Kat laughed, flailing about, making faces at the corny music, and cracking me up. I decided that the best strategy would be to imitate a person falling from a building, and this seemed to produce a series of spastic yet wholly appropriate dance moves.

Jerry stood in a corner, eating from a bucket of Kentucky Fried Chicken carried under his arm, pretending to study a fire code bulletin on the wall. Kat noticed him before I did. Her hand went to her throat. We hurried to the opposite side of the hall, to the foyer by the restrooms.

"Oh my God, what is he doing here?" Kat gasped. "He wasn't invited. How did he know?"

"I don't know," I said. "Maybe he'll just leave."

We watched Jerry from behind a pillar. George and Veronica were still dancing and laughing; they hadn't noticed him. Jerry walked slowly around the perimeter of the room, then left through an exit.

"Maybe he won't come back," I said. "Maybe he's uncomfortable." But then he reappeared through the same door, tearing meat off a drumstick with his teeth, bobbing his head a bit to the music. I watched Veronica notice him and register his presence, a jolt rattling her body; she hissed some frantic words into George's ear. While she walked briskly off the dance floor, past us, into the ladies' room, George located two of the groomsmen and quickly informed them of the unwanted guest. There were quick nods, the no-bullshit exchanges of men going into action. Almost casually, the groomsmen approached Jerry, who had wandered over to the gift table. One of the groomsmen said something and Jerry looked up, sort of quizzically, then looked at the other groomsman, gestured to the dance floor, and said something. There were more words from the groomsmen. Jerry shook his head, said something more emphatically. One of the groomsmen tried to take his arm but Jerry jerked away, barking something I could almost hear over the music, then walked to the side of the room where the food was. By now more guests had become aware of the unwanted guest and were conferring over the lips of beer bottles and tiny plates of toothpicked cheese as to his identity. I watched the mortification of their expressions as they realized, suddenly, that this was

Veronica's ex-husband. Kat left my side and disappeared into the bathroom to find her mother. The band started in on the chicken song, advising everyone to flap their arms at incrementally lower elevations. Jerry went on eating his drumstick and George marched past me with his graying, balding best man, saying "The cops is what I'm going to do. I'm not going to let that guy fuck up my wedding. How the *hell* did he know about this? Shit, shit, shit."

"I'm on it, George. Don't worry. We'll take care of this asshole," the best man said, as though this kind of thing was a standard expectation of duty for the male half of a wedding party.

The three groomsmen approached Jerry and attempted to take him by the arms. The band kept playing, but only children and a couple clueless elderly people were still trying to perform the chicken dance. Jerry reached into the KFC bucket and came up with a gun.

The band slowed down and the microphone went into a spasm of feedback. The bassist continued for a couple bars and the drummer couldn't resist a final fill. Then the music ceased, leaving the entire All-Purpose Hall in silence. Jerry said, "I'm not here to cause any problems. I just want to say a few words to the groom."

The band's abrupt halt drew Kat and Veronica from the ladies' room. Veronica stumbled and maybe she understood what was about to happen. I was closest to her, so she grabbed onto my arm and leaned beside me against the pillar. "What's he doing? My God, what's happening?" she said.

A guest said, "Hey, what happened to the music? I was just starting to get groovy."

"Which one of you guys in the penguin suits is the groom?" Jerry said.

George stepped forward and said, "I'm Veronica's husband, and I'm asking you to leave."

"Nice. Well, okay, I just wanted to say congratulations. Cool your jets, I'm not here to ruin anything, I even brought my own grub."

"Please, just leave."

Jerry walked to the center of the deserted dance floor and took the mic from the singer, who recoiled and shuffled behind the drum set.

"Well, I usually don't speak in front of crowds so bear with me," Jerry said. "I think a toast is in order. And it's time to cut the cake. Go on, head over to the cake."

"Jerry don't do this!" Veronica pleaded.

"I said cut the *fucking cake*!"

A couple kids started crying, and those grown-ups who had their senses headed for the doors. Shaking, George took Veronica by the arm and together they painfully trudged to the cake. Kat's new manicure dug into my arm.

"All right, all you AA folks I guess are going to have to toast with apple cider or something, but let's crack open some of that champagne, what do you say? Hey! It's my old buddy, Cedar! Say, do me a favor and start popping some of them corks, will you now?"

Everyone looked at me. Blood abandoned Kat's fingers, leaving them cold against my skin. "You told him," she whispered.

I walked across the floor as if I were walking across the deck of a listing ship. Somehow I arrived at the table with the cake. I struggled with a couple bottles, poured the champagne into glasses. Veronica stood with her eyes closed, her back to Jerry, mumbling something I couldn't hear, a prayer maybe. A little boy asked his mother if there would be ice cream with the cake. Jerry told me to start handing out glasses. I followed the commands of the man with the gun until all the remaining, shell-shocked guests had their bubbly. I wondered if anyone had tried calling the police.

"Super," Jerry said, "now I guess you're all wondering why I showed up tonight, on such a joyous occasion. I came to give a toast. To long lasting love!" He raised his glass. When no one else did, he yelled, "Raise your fucking glasses!"

Guests mumbled cheers and clinked glasses. Jerry poured himself some more. "Now the bride, she's a piece of work, isn't she? Used to let her sell blow jobs when we needed the extra cash. True story. No fucking, just head. That was our little arrangement. And now look at her. All done up like a big fucking birthday present. Who are you trying to kid, baby? Aw, crying on your own wedding day. How touching. Well babe, I raise my glass to your eternal happiness." Jerry raised his glass again, then banged the butt of the gun on the table. "Come on, you fucks! When I say toast we're all gonna toast or I swear to God I'll blow someone's fucking heart out!"

"Here, here!" one of the groomsmen said.

"That's the spirit. Finally, I'd like to raise a glass in honor of the groom. Oops, looks like he's just pissed himself. Is this a classy wedding or what? To the man who fucked my daughter. To the man who knocked her up. To the man who made my little girl get an abortion." Jerry drained the contents of his glass, then tossed it aside. He pushed the gun away from his body. There was supposed to be something exciting happening here, but what struck me most was a sense of deep embarrassment, like watching a mentally retarded person come unglued in public. Utterly incapable and petrified, I responded in the most inappropriate manner possible; I *laughed*. I expected George to cower or beg for his life or deny the accusation but the shooting didn't play out like this. What rose through this tall man with a new bride was anger unlike any I'd seen. His knuckles popped as he turned them into fists and every inch of him seemed to vibrate with rage. He took a step forward and pointed his finger. The words passing his lips twisted his face into a scowl menacing and feral. "*You will not hurt the ones I love.*"

I expected the gun to sound louder, and almost believed it was fake, a prop in an elaborate and twisted joke. But that was real blood sprayed on Veronica's wedding dress, those were real screaming people around me, and a real wounded man contorted his prone body on a floor where minutes before people had been dancing the chicken dance. This wasn't *cool* or *redemptive* or *cathartic* or any of the shit movies make you feel about violence. This was sick, and I was still sickly laughing. I think I fainted for a bit, or at least didn't notice everyone running for the doors, and when I pulled my head away from the pillar the room was emptied of wedding guests. Veronica was holding George's head, rocking on the floor, wailing. George's mouth opened and closed like a fish. Jerry sat nearby, on a rented folding chair, calmly eating a piece of cake from a plastic plate. Three cops materialized in the doorway, guns drawn; one of them Officer Stoner. There was some hands-up type language and some threats, the barked orders of officers who rarely saw this category of mayhem. Jerry shrugged, stuffed another forkful of white cake into his face. Mouth oozing with frosting, he rammed in the barrel and scattered his brain out the back of his head. He rocked backward and for a moment it appeared that the chair would tip over and spill him onto the floor. The chair wobbled on its back legs as if waiting for Jerry to die before it toppled, but as the echoes of the shot dissipated, the chair righted itself, ably supporting the dead man.

Albany.

It was a little after six in the morning. Kat appeared to be sleeping facedown, fully clothed, with boots on, on my bed. I needed to brush my teeth. I brushed for about five minutes, slowly, letting toothpaste fall out of my mouth in foamy plops.

"The story about the boy you met on your trip was true, wasn't it?"

From the other room, Kat replied, "Yes."

I spit into the sink. "You let me believe George did it."

"You would have been disappointed to learn he hadn't."

"You hated George anyway, so you just let me think the worst about the guy. As a kind of revenge," I said.

"That sounds plausible."

"You met some kid in a seaside town, slept with him, and that was it."

Kat messed with the room's miniature coffee maker. "He wasn't really a kid. More like in his twenties. He said he worked on fishing boats in the summer and snow-boarded in the winter. He'd made enough money to buy a boat of his own. I spent the rest of the vacation debating whether to tell you. When you came to a conclusion on your own I let it stick. I'm really sorry, Cedar."

The coffee maker struggled to life, forcing hot water through a presealed packet of stale grounds. We watched it drip as snow turned to slush outside.

"What do you say we get the hell out of here and find somewhere with real breakfast?" I said.

"There's a Denny's just up the road."

"Let's do it. I'll meet you at your room in ten."

Outside, bundled and walking precariously through the whitened parking lot, I felt free of the stifling innards of the motel room and Kat's narrative. I appreciated the bracing cold, the condensation on my glasses. We trudged through tire tracks, across parking lots, to the roadside Denny's. Inside, we enmeshed ourselves in the flow of truckers and other snowed-in travelers, got seated in a booth, and were soon enjoying coffee a little stronger than the crap that had been brewed in my room. This was the kind of place where crummy weather outside made the food taste better. I was hungry for eggs. I wanted an American breakfast with all the fat, cholesterol, and starch it implied. I ordered extra sausage on the side. I ordered the tall stack. I asked the waitress for a refill on coffee. Kat ate a cinnamon roll and devoured a yogurt-and-fruit cup. I needed a shave, but I didn't give a fuck. I reached over and touched Kat's hand as it made for the cream.

"It's okay about that guy on the boat. I don't care. I don't even care you lied about it."

"I almost didn't go through with the abortion."

"Yeah, I mean, you debated about it."

"I was scared. A couple days before we went to the clinic, I tracked down Father Roth to ask his advice."

"No kidding."

Kat nodded. "I made up an excuse and took the ferry into the city. I went to that church where my mom and I used to go the AA meetings, and asked someone there, an official of some sort, a deacon, if I could see Father Roth. He hadn't been with that church for a while. But they knew his full name. Desmond Roth. I went to a phone booth and looked him up. I called and an old man answered. When I asked for Father Roth he laughed and said Father Roth was long gone. When I asked for Desmond he said it was him. I told him I was a former member of his church and had something very important I needed to discuss with him. He tried brushing me off, saying he was no longer a priest but I begged and he finally agreed to meet me. He actually didn't live that far from the church, ten blocks or something.

"So I showed up at this condo. You know how it goes, seeing people you haven't seen a while. There's this moment when you first see them when you try to fit them into your old memory. He looked a hundred years old. He was thin and balding and his breath smelled, literally, like shit. His skin looked all scabby and his eyes were sunken in and surrounded by these harried black bags. I would have turned and ran if he hadn't shaken his finger at me, smiled, and said he remembered me.

"So I followed him through this mess of dead house-plants and cardboard boxes, into his place. All the blinds were down. A TV was playing a soap opera, if I remember. A parakeet was screeching. It was afternoon now and I noticed he was still in his pj's and bath robe. It stank even more like shit, like human shit, beyond a bad bathroom smell, it was just horrid. But my disgust quickly faded and I started feeling real pity for the man. He was on his last legs, I could tell. He almost fell, sitting down in his chair in the kitchen. I asked him if he wanted me to make him some tea and he didn't say no. So I put the water on to boil and got a pretty good look at the refrigerator, which had all these pictures on the door of Father Roth on various vacations with these other guys, everyone tanned and happy in the sun. At one point he went into a hellish coughing fit and the water wouldn't boil fast enough to make the tea. Finally he calmed down and said he was sorry I had to visit him in such a squalid place.

"I was trying to just make conversation before I got on with my big questions, so I asked what made him decide to leave the church. I was starting to make the connection that the reasons were, you know, sexual. He said—and I remember this exactly—'I was tired of being judged a sinner by men who raped little boys.' Apparently, he had come out to his bishop, basically told him he wanted to spend his life with another man and didn't want to hide it. Soon after that he was defrocked.

"After I made him his tea, he started babbling about all sorts of things, but one thing he said stuck with me. He said suffering is the only true barometer of the health of the spirit. He said Christianity is flawed because it's a belief system based on the avoidance of sin rather than relieving suffering. This was one of the opinions he picked up after he was defrocked, when he started studying the world's religions. He traveled through South America and Asia for a year with a nondenominational group that gave prosthetic limbs to land-mine victims. He came back with a boyfriend from Buenos Aires and they broke up within a couple months. He said he went through a real rough patch where he tried to kill himself, actually cut his wrist in the bathtub enough to make himself faint, but luckily a friend found him."

"AIDS?" I asked.

"Of course. But his problems were bigger than a disease. So, I told him I had gotten pregnant and was considering an abortion. I asked him if I was going to hell." Kat flagged down a waitress. "Ma'am? I could use more coffee, please?"

She turned back to me. "You were always an atheist. I became one the hard way."

"I've just never trusted the medical opinions of people who believe the world is four thousand years old," I said.

The waitress filled up our mugs, throwing off our sugar/cream ratios.

I said, "So what did Father Roth say? When you asked him if you were going to hell?"

"He told me that God is the world's most prolific abortionist."

Outside snow plows had cleared the road to the airport. I started thinking about flights and ground transportation. We finished breakfast and lumbered back to the motel, our conversation devolving into the small talk of people about to say good-bye. I made arrangements to catch a flight scheduled to leave in about four hours, took a shower, put on my least dirty clothes, and glanced at the primary colors of a complimentary *USA Today*. Kat walked into my room without knocking and handed me the final pages of her manuscript.

"This is the end," she said before she kissed me.

Acknowledgments

The author would like to thank the following people and organizations for their kindness, generosity, and support.

Jennifer Beard, Miles Boudinot, Scarlett Boudinot.

Aimee Bender, Rick Moody, Matthew Simmons, Suzanne Stockman, Rebecca Brown, Sherman Alexie.

Everyone at the Richard Hugo House, New City Theater, the Goddard College Port Townsend MFA program, and Planned Parenthood.

Dave Cornelius.

PJ Mark, Amy Hundley, and everyone at Grove/Atlantic, Inc.

Misconception

Ryan Boudinot

ABOUT THIS GUIDE

We hope that these discussion questions
will enhance your reading group's exploration
of Ryan Boudinot's *Misconception*. They are meant
to stimulate discussion, offer new viewpoints and
enrich your enjoyment of the book.

More reading group guides and additional information, including summaries, author tours and author
sites for other fine Grove Press titles may be found
on our Web site, www.groveatlantic.com.

QUESTIONS FOR DISCUSSION

1. Many authors have explored the role of memory in storytelling. Lewis Carroll wrote in *Through the Looking Glass* "It's a poor sort of memory that only works backwards." With that in mind think about memory in Ryan Boudinot's novel. How does it work?

2. In how many ways does the title, *Misconception,* relate to the story? Can you find various meanings? What is your understanding of misconception? What do you think of the subtitle? Did it affect your perception as you read? Did it make itself clear in the end?

3. Most novels are written in first person or third person. Boudinot has woven two first person narratives into an inventive work. Who wrote the first chapter? Why? What are the differences in Kat's and Cedar's narratives? Is it more than just different voices? What is the nature of truth in memory?

4. Almost everything we know about Janet and Wade Rivers is written by Kat. How do you think that Cedar would describe them? Did it surprise you when they decided to separate? Did it surprise Cedar?

5. What is Kat conveying when she says that she has "moved across the mountains to the green side?" (p. 49). How does this affect her reaction to George's proposed RV vacation later on? Did you find Kat's description of the trip sad or funny or both and what does this reflect about the character of George?

6. "I was happiest en route, with my laptop and a coffee in a sleeved paper cup, arranging ground transportation, stepping from the gate to plane to gate. Inhaling jet fumes in the optimism of rental-car parking lots" (p. 33). What does this tell you about the adult Cedar? Did you think that he had changed from the adolescent Cedar?

7. "In Kat's hotel room, I stepped over a case of wine and cleared a half-finished Sunday *Times* crossword from a chair. She offered an insincere apology for the mess. On the desk were the contents of a sack lunch: a cellophane-wrapped sandwich, an apple, carrot sticks. Some books—*In Cold Blood*, something by Philip Roth. Her clothes all over the place. On the table sat a Power-Book. Toilet articles and coffee supplies, a printer, a sleeping bag, CDs in sleeves, masking tape. Loose change. A lone tampon clawing its way out of its applicator. A pack of spearmint gum" (p. 39). What sort of picture did this assortment of stuff show you? Did it match with your impressions of the young Kat?

8. In the chapter narrated by Kat—the manuscript of her memoir that Cedar is reading—Kat is an inexperienced pre-adolescent. What does she understand about her mother? What effects does her friendship with Margot have upon her?

9. "Cedar Rivers is a boy in my class who we call the Mad Scientist" (p. 59). How does Kat feel about Cedar at this point? When she is telling of the same incidents in Cedar's voice in the first chapter, is she trying to give a different impression?

10. What did you think of the device of Cedar finding Kat's book of short stories, *Nymphonomicom*, on Amazon .com along with the self-consciously erudite review written by Ryan Boudinot?

11. "'You get to see parts of bodies that the bodies themselves never saw.' 'Like a memoir. You get to see parts of lives that those living them never saw'" (p. 73). What makes this exchange between the grown-up physician, Cedar and the writer, Kat so poignant?

12. "We spotted Kat's father's van—a white beaten-up Ford with the name of his employer, Apex Septic, stenciled crappily on the side—across the street in the KFC parking lot. A man appeared to be sleeping inside. The

tailgate bore an ideology in the form of a bumper sticker: Bosses are like diapers. *Full of shit and always on your ass!!!!*" (p. 77). What does the meeting between Jerry and Kat at Kentucky Fried Chicken reveal about Kat's connection to her father? Why does she want Cedar to come along? What does Cedar fail to notice about Jerry?

13. "We laughed. Veronica's boyfriend, George, clomped stiffly up the stairs. He was an angular format of human being with tiny eyes in the kind of bald head that seems to automatically come with a mustache" (p. 23). What are Kat's feelings about her perspective step-father, George? What does Cedar fail to notice about George?

14. Do you think that Jerry and Veronica make an improbable couple? In the chapter Santa Cruz 1970, describing their meeting and courtship, what drew the two to each other?

15. "George hesitated then touched Kat's shoulder. She shrugged him off. 'Don't touch me. Pervert'" (p. 99). When Cedar witnesses this interaction, he takes it as further proof that George has raped Kat. But Cedar assumed this from the beginning—why? Do you think it ever crossed Cedar's mind that Kat might have been

unfaithful, or would he rather believe that she had been raped? And when do you (as a reader) realize that he is wrong?"

16. "As I stared through my smudged reflection at the landscape, I had no idea how I was going to find Kat's father, or where I would stay that night. The Greyhound deposited me at the station" (p. 133). In the chapter Beyond Mountains, Cedar sets out on a quest. "'I'm not a runaway. I always meant to come back. I'm not like the other kids who come in here. I don't do drugs, I get good grades. I'm studying medical text books on my own because I'm going to be a doctor.' 'And you needed to go on a little road trip to find someone.' 'Yeah, I needed to find my—' I stopped" (p. 150). What emotions does he unconsciously express to Mr. Cox?

17. "You think you know everything about me. You think you can see inside my head. But you have no *clue* what I'm about. You barged into my life and started thinking you had authority over it. That thing that happened to me, I wish I had never told you about it. I wish I'd just taken care of it myself" (p. 159). Kat makes this dramatic statement at the end of Beyond Mountains. Think about the implications. What is really happening between Cedar and Kat?

18. "I. Hate. Boys" (p. 163). In Kat's three-page screed about the opposite sex, what is she trying to clarify? Why won't she allow George to be kind to her? Why is it impossible for her to understand her mother's justifications for marrying George?

19. Do you think that George and Veronica make an improbable couple? What do you imagine happened after all the revelations at George and Veronica's dramatic wedding?

20. "I said, 'so what did Father Roth say? When you asked him if you were going to hell?' 'He told me that God is the world's most prolific abortionist'" (p. 214). Were you surprised by Kat's final revelations to Cedar? In the end, why do you think she wanted to see Cedar again and for him to read her book?

SUGGESTIONS FOR FURTHER READING

Franny and Zooey by J.D. Salinger; *Downtown Owl* by Chuck Klosterman; *The Brief Wondrous Life of Oscar Wao* by Junot Díaz; *The Ice Storm* by Rick Moody; *The Rotters Club* by Jonathan Coe; *The Autograph Man* by Zadie Smith; *Special Topics in Calamity Physics* by Marisha Pessl; *A Heartbreaking Work of Staggering Genius* by Dave Eggers

SUGGESTIONS FOR FILMS

Juno; The Royal Tenenbaums; Memento; Eternal Sunshine of the Spotless Mind